Dedication

I dedicate my *first* book to all authors. Books have inspired me, comforted me, and encouraged me my entire life. The characters that were brought to life, the places they helped my mind to travel, and the words they helped my tongue learn, were a blessing. Books allow you to daydream and disconnect from reality for a few hours. Thank you to all authors who provide this gift. Thank you to those who inspired me to share my imagination.

Prologue

Andrea hurried down the street, doing what she knew she shouldn't, even as she felt compelled to do it anyway. She was texting while walking...or trying her hardest to. She was running late, and the sidewalk was crowded with the lunch hour rush of bodies. Mika was going to fuss at her, since she was usually the one admonishing her friend about being late all the time. Add to that, she was trying to reply back to an annoying work email from a co-worker that always worked her nerves. So it was a given, she would eventually bump into someone.

However, she hadn't thought it would feel like a brick wall when she did. Smothering the curse that almost escaped, she stumbled backwards, grappling with her phone and balance, as firm hands steadied her by the waist.

She looked up to see who she would be apologizing to, even though she was unreasonably irritated. When she met a pair of light brown eyes set in a handsome brown face, it was almost enough to make her pause. The amused smile on a pair of perfectly full lips *certainly* did.

"Whoa there, are you okay?"

"Sorry about that. I was on my stupid phone and wasn't paying attention." She stepped back from his hands and he blinked, as if he had just realized he was still touching her.

"I understand. I hate how uneducated phones are now days."

"What?" She tried taking another step back into the jostling crowd. Apparently, gorgeous eyes hid a mentally defective mind.

"It's a joke...apparently a bad one," he commented. Putting one hand high on her waist, he navigated her to the side, closer to the shop windows and out of the crowd's way.

"Oh." Frown lines marred her forehead. "Okay..."

"You said your phone was stupid, I ran with it."

"Oh!" She actually gave a small laugh. "I get it now, though that *is* a terrible joke." Not to mention her mind had been elsewhere, like on those kissable lips that were smiling at her again.

"No problem. Like I said, I understand. You should be careful though, you can really hurt yourself walking and texting like that."

"I know. I usually don't. Thanks for being a good sport." They stood there for another few seconds, staring at each other in silence. "I should get going."

"If you have another minute, I'd love to get your number. I'd like to take you out when you have some free time."

Another pregnant pause as Andrea's mind raced. She didn't even know his name! "I, uh...I don't usually give out my number. I mean, I don't even know you."

"Cam, Cam Holden." He held out his hand. "A pleasure to meet you."

She found herself instinctively reaching out to shake his hand, and that's when she felt a little jolt of electricity travel from her palm to her wrist. She could tell he felt it too, as those gorgeous brown eyes widened.

Cam shook his head as if to clear it. "And your name is?" His voice came out lower. It seemed the spark they'd felt affected more body parts than just his hand.

"Andrea," she said softly, then a little louder. "Andrea Cole."

"Andrea Cole," he said slowly, as if he was tasting the sound of her name on his tongue.

Clearing her throat, she gave a gentle tug, realizing they were still holding hands. He resisted for a moment before letting go.

"Look Andrea, since you don't feel comfortable giving me your number, let me give you mine." He reached into his computer bag, pulling out a business card and pen. He took a moment to write and then handed it over to her. "That's my personal number on the back. Think about it and give me a call when you feel comfortable. I'd love to take you out and get to know you."

"I'll think about it...no promises." She put the card in her purse and looked back up to see him smiling at her.

"You have really pretty eyes, did you know that?"

"What?" She frowned at him again as he stepped past her chuckling.

Cam departed with one last comment. "Walk safe, pretty eyes."

Chapter One

Andrea walked into the restaurant and made a beeline for their table. They had a standing lunch date every other Friday. The medium sized café was happy to save a table for them. She sat down as Mika wrapped up her phone conversation and pointed a finger at her.

"*You* Ms. Cole, are late. You better have a good excuse."

Andrea took a deep breath and huffed out, "I met a man." She smirked as Mika's mouth dropped open.

"*You* met a man? Well, that is the best excuse ever. Give me the when, what, where and how."

"Three minutes ago. We had a brief convo that ended with me getting his number. I met him on the sidewalk coming here, while I was emailing on my phone."

Mika was delayed in responding as the waitress brought over their order. When that was done, she tilted her curly head and fired off the rest of her questions. "Was he cute?"

"Yes...very."

"Was he at least six inches taller than you?"

Andrea rolled her eyes at one of Mika's dating rules. "How the heck should I know? I don't carry a tape measure with me. I'd say he was about 6'1."

"That works, you're only 5'6. Does he have a job?"

"I'm 5'6 and a half, get it right. Yes, he has a job per the business card he gave me." Andrea tossed the card down on the table.

"Good, good." Mika took a look at the card. "Camden Holden...is he black?"

Andrea snatched the card back. "What difference does it make? I've told you I date all races."

"Wrong." She pointed her straw at Andrea. "You don't date anyone."

"Hey, that's not true!"

"It is too! You haven't been on one single date in the last six months."

"That can't be right." They both cut off the conversation as their salads were brought out. Andrea wrinkled her forehead as she thought back to the last date she'd had. *It had been...well it had to be...had it really been six months?*

As if Mika could read her mind, she answered, "Yes, it's been six months."

"What are you, my stalker or something?"

"Heffa please! As if you're good enough for me to stalk. What I *am* is your best friend. I remember stuff like your last date, especially since they happen so rarely."

"Whatever. Eat your damn salad." They ate quietly for a few minutes, before she glanced up to see Mika staring at her. "What?"

"So, are you going to call him?"

She paused with her fork halfway to her mouth. She'd been in shock as he left her with the compliment about her eyes. No man had ever complimented her on what she thought were plain, dark brown orbs. Those thoughts had carried her to the restaurant, where she was now being interrogated. "I doubt it."

"Why in the world not?"

"I mean, I met him on the sidewalk."

"So?"

"So, it was the sidewalk."

"Now who has snobby dating rules?" Mika grinned at her exasperated friend. "I'd say a sidewalk is technically better than a club where half the folks are drunk. So cross that off your excuse list. Next!"

6

"Ugh...I don't really have time..."

"Nope, nope, nope. I refuse to hear that nonsense. You have plenty of time. Besides work and hanging with me, you don't do much else."

"Hey! I take offense to that. I have other friends. I do stuff!"

"Mmm-hmm. Sure you do. Even so, you have enough time to give a few hours to a cute, black, employed, tallish man."

"He was more than tall enough," Andrea defended.

Mika threw up her hands. "Okay, so what's your problem?"

"Dating...is so much trouble."

"You kill me. You act like you entering a two year contract with T-Mobile. It's just you picking up the phone and going on a date *or* two with a guy."

"I don't know, I'm not sure I should take him seriously."

"Why, what did he do?"

"He...dropped a line on me. Told me I had pretty eyes."

Mika just shook her head as their main meal arrived and studied her friend of six years. Andrea was what she considered an "under-estimator" when it came to herself. She was a literal type of person, so she often failed to see anything that wasn't plainly in front of her. "Why would you think that's a line? Even if it was, would it be such a bad one? At least he didn't make a crude remark about your chest or ass. You *do* have pretty eyes."

"No, *you* have pretty eyes, *he* had pretty eyes, *I* have plain eyes."

"Not true, you have dark brown eyes with flicks of visible light brown around your iris, which make your eyes pop. It's not odd that a man would think them pretty."

Andrea took a long sip of her water. She'd never noticed that about her eyes. "Still..."

"Still nothing. He sounds like a nice guy, noticing something like that. Sounds like a guy who deserves at least a call."

Still not convinced, Andrea attacked her burger and fries, making the small salad she'd just eaten pointless. "We'll see."

"Call him."

"I said we'll see."

Mika let it go, as she knew Andrea had a stubborn streak that could rival her own. They finished the meal by talking about the work week and the weekend ahead. Thirty-five minutes later they walked out the café together, preparing to walk back to their offices, which were in opposite directions.

"So you gone call him or what?"

"I told you, I'll see."

Mika looked at her seriously and reached out to touch her shoulder. "Sorry to be such an ass about this, but honestly I'm worried about you. Six months...not one single date. You are too young to be out of the dating game."

"I'm older than you remember."

"By just a year! I don't consider myself done with dating yet."

"I know, I know! I told you I'd think about it." Andrea gave her a brief hug before pulling back. "Can you be satisfied with that and stop clucking like a mother hen? You date enough for both of us."

"I can share the details of my dating adventures, but the one thing I *can't* share, is actual penis. You should look into getting some of *that*, every once in a while."

"Shut up!" Andrea laughed and shooed her away.

"I'm just saying!" Mika started walking. "Give him a call! What could it hurt?"

Andrea shook her head and waved goodbye. As she made her way back to the office, she thought on her friendship with Mika. They had meet six years ago, when she was twenty-two in her last year of college at Wayne State, and Mika was twenty-one. They'd both been doing a year long rotational internship at Ernst & Young. They had been sitting in orientation listening to everyone do their introductions. Unsurprisingly they were the only two black women in the group of twelve. A white girl stood up front talking, her skirt tight, smile extra bright and in general, giving off that "dumb blond who will make it far" vibe. They'd suddenly glanced at each other and rolled their eyes.

From that day forward, they had become fast friends. Supporting each other through the micro-aggressions of being young, black, and in an ultra-professional setting. They'd partied together even though they went to different schools. Celebrating all the milestones of their lives, professional and personal. And now, as they both rounded up to thirty, they were still holding tight as friends.

The problem was her friend believed in taking way more chances in her personal life than Andrea did. Truth be told, she'd poured most of her energy into her career at this point. She'd had *real* relationships over the years. One in high school, one in college, and one after college. That one had lasted a full year, ending when she realized her happily ever after of a marriage proposal would not be happening. That failure had left her really hurt. She could admit, that since then her relationships if they could be called that, had usually lasted three to six months. In the last year or so, it was rare if she got past three dates with a guy.

She didn't really believe in causal hook-ups either. Sleeping with someone for sex, with no other connection had never appealed to her. Yet lately, she hadn't found anyone who kept her interest long enough, to where she felt comfortable getting physical with them. That was why

Mika's question wasn't easy to answer. That instant spark, attraction, whatever you wanted to call it, had been jarring. She had a feeling tangling with Camden Holden *could* hurt a lot.

Chapter Two

Cam sat at one of his favorite bars waiting on Robert to arrive. He had finished up his work early, not surprising since he hadn't been able to concentrate for shit. His thoughts wandering often to the beautiful woman he'd met on the street. She had the prettiest brown skin and those pretty dark brown eyes that sparkled with flecks of cinnamon. But it was that smile that she'd only graced him with once which made him feel like he'd won a prize.

It wasn't unusual for Cam to work outside of his home. As an independent graphic, web, and content designer, he could work from anywhere. When the weather was nice, he often would come downtown and pick an outside spot to work. He was taking advantage of the end of August weather. Since it was Michigan the weather could change on a dime. Even when fall and winter rolled in, he would often come down and pick one of the many small shops to work in. Detroit in the last few years, had increased its co-operative work spaces, so he could take advantage of those as well.

He owned a cheap two-story, four bedroom house right outside of the official down town area. When he'd purchased the house, it had been *just shy* of being a rundown property, but not so much that he couldn't move in right away. He and Robert had done most of the basic repairs, then he'd paid a local electrician do some much needed updates to the wiring. With his type of business, the house definitely needed to be brought into the twenty-first century. Being a tech savvy guy, he wanted his home to have all the electronic bells and whistles. He was happy to plant his roots where he'd grown up. He believed in helping black neighborhoods and with the gentrification going on, every black body was needed. At the same time, he loved that downtown had started to thrive, so he liked to spend his time and money here as much as possible.

Through the window, he finally spotted Robert approaching. Most Fridays, they had drinks at the end of the day. Cam pushed the ritual, more as a way to get Robert to leave work on time, at least *once* a week. He'd met Robert the first year he'd moved back to Michigan, after completing his Master's at Duke University. He'd been working on a four month project at the company Robert worked for, and the man had been in some of the project meetings. Robert had been pretty chilly towards him until he'd found out Cam was originally from the "D".

They'd started with a few beers after work, and found they had enough in common to make them friends. They were both really focused, just in different ways. Both were young black men determined to live life on their own terms, different though they may be. They both respected what they saw in the other. Drive, determination, and someone who got results. Now the friend who was more like a brother to him, took a seat at the table.

Robert signaled their usual waitress to come over. They ordered and he made sure to get a beer in his hand before he focused on Cam. "Man, sorry I'm a little late."

"No, you cool, I was early today."

"You ran out of ideas or something?"

"Naw, never that my brother." Cam grinned at him. "I've been struggling since lunch."

Now Robert paid closer attention. "What? You got creator's block or something? That's fairly unusual for you, unless you got a client being nit-picky."

"I almost wish it was a client. Would be easier to handle. I met a woman on my way back from lunch, and let's just say she's been on my mind ever since."

Robert's usually restrained expression turned animated. "That sounds like a good problem to me. She must have been real fine to keep you that unfocused."

"She probably was. I didn't get past her eyes and smile."

"Man what?" Robert laughed "You been struck by lightning or something?"

Cam cracked a wry smile. "You could say that. Man when we touched, I swear I *did* feel electricity."

"Get the fuck out!" Robert would have kept going but he choked on his beer, and it took him almost two minutes to get under control. He couldn't believe what he was hearing. Out of the two of them, Camden was the one who barely got serious about a woman. He liked to play the field. Oh he was honest with them, and only went for those who were looking for someone to hang out with. Dates, outings, and if both parties were into it bed room sport. But he had never heard Cam talk about a woman like he was today. "So, you gone sit there and not even ask me if I'm all right?"

Cam just crossed his arms and leaned back in his chair, pointing a finger. "That's what you get for laughing at me."

"Okay, okay, my bad. So now I got to know what exactly happened with this lady of yours."

Cam sat forward again, eager like a boy who had new comics to share. "That's the thing, not much did happen. I was walking down the sidewalk, and she literally ran into me."

"Did she knock you down so you hit your head?"

"No, I can't explain it. All I did was steady her, talk for a few minutes, and ask her could I get her number." He paused for effect. "She didn't give it to me."

"And that has you grinning like an idiot?"

Cam shook his head and shrugged. "She took my number at least."

"So let me get this straight. You talking about her eyes and smile, not her ass mind you. Yet you have no idea if you'll ever talk to her again, much less see her. Do I have that right?"

Cam just shrugged again and grinned at his perplexed friend.

"Are you sure you didn't hit your head?"

"No, it was just something about her." Cam played with his beer glass, pushing it from side to side on the table.

"Right. So what if she doesn't call?"

"Then...I guess that will be that."

"Mmm, well it's curious to see you take an interest in someone."

Cam frowned. "What is that supposed to mean?"

Now it was Robert's turn to shrug. He could tell he'd touched a nerve. "Just saying. Seems like this woman...hold up, did you even get her name?"

"Yeah, Andrea."

"Okay, it seems like this Andrea really caught your attention is all."

"Well it's not *that* big of a deal. If she calls, she calls. If she doesn't, she doesn't."

Robert opened his mouth to respond, but luckily for Cam their food arrived. While they were being served, Cam wondered why Robert's comment bothered him so much. It wasn't like he was *sweating* over this woman. He'd only talked to her for a few minutes! It wasn't a big deal...at least not to him.

Robert thanked the waitress as she left, since Cam seemed like he was in his own world. Something about this Andrea had his friend uneasy. This was going to be very, very interesting. He decided to let it go for now. He had a feeling there would be plenty of time to rib his friend about this subject later.

As they ate Cam talked about his latest project, then Robert changed the topic to sports, his favorite subject outside of finances. He let the easy conversation with his friend push thoughts of dark brown eyes, out of his mind. They stayed until a little after nine, before Robert gave him a lift to his house a few miles away. He'd walked and taken the QLine earlier in the day.

"Thanks for the ride man. You want to come in and chill?" Cam asked as he cracked open the car door.

"No, I'm good. It was a rough week. I'm about to go home and crash."

"Cool, I'll holla at you later."

Cam was fully out of the car before Robert called out, "Hey, Camden?"

Cam warily turned around. Robert only used his full name when he was up to something. "Yeah, what?"

"Let's place a little bet on whether your Andrea contacts you or not."

"Man what? You tripping. It's not even that deep."

"So you keep saying. If it's no big deal one way or the other, bet fifty."

Cam narrowed his eyes in irritation. "You got money to waste like that?"

Robert's grin grew. "Of course I do. It's why I invest, just so I can make bets with you."

"Fine. Whatever." Cam shut the door harder than normal, only to hear laughter through the open window.

"So, I get fifty if she doesn't reach out within two weeks, and I'll pay you fifty if she does."

"I said whatever. Fifty is it. Gone and take your old man, sleepy ass home," Cam said irritably. He walked away, still hearing laughter as the car reversed out the drive.

Chapter Three

Andrea was taking her lunch in her office with the door shut. She rarely closed her door, but she deserved a real break after immersing herself in work this week. For probably the twentieth time, she played with Camden Holden's business card. Of course, she'd checked out his website to make sure he was legit. Anyone could make business cards. She had to admit, he did good work. With a sigh, she tossed the card on her desk and learned back in her chair.

She didn't know why she hadn't thrown it away by now. She didn't have time to tangle with some guy at the moment. Every time she was on the verge of tossing it, the fact that she *hadn't* actually had a date in six months would make her hesitate. She knew it wasn't usual for women her age not to date. Women close to being thirty, hormones usually went into an overactive phase, trying to snag a husband before the big 3-0. Shaking her head, she focused on whether or not she even *wanted* a date. Sitting forward, she picked up his card and emailed him a short message before she could overthink it.

Hi, it's Andrea, the lady who tried to mow you over. I just wanted to check that I didn't do any lasting damage. Have a good day.

She hit the send button before she could change her mind. She sat back and chewed on the top of her pen, a nasty habit she had started in middle school and never entirely shed. Should she have said, *"I hope to hear from you soon?"* Phrasing it that way implied expectations.

Maybe he was a natural flirt and never meant to really take her out. Maybe she had waited too long to contact him. With a sigh of disgust, she tossed her pen down and prepared to get back to work. Just then, her work phone rang.

"Hello, Andrea Cole speaking. How may I help you?"

"Andrea...it's Cam."

She straightened up so quick, her chair started to roll back. "Oh Camden! I didn't expect you to call." What she really meant was that she hadn't expected to hear from him at all...*ever.*

"I hope you don't mind. I got your email and assumed you might still be at your desk. Though I suppose you could have been walking and texting again. Running into unsuspecting men."

Relaxing back, she laughed. "No, I swear I've reformed my ways. I won't cause sidewalk disasters again."

"It wasn't a disaster. It was a very good day for me...I met you."

Andrea's brain froze. That was a very direct statement. "Well..."

"I was happy to get your email. I was starting to think you wouldn't reach out."

"I almost didn't. I mean...I've been busy."

"Hmm, I bet. So, does this mean you'll let me to take you out after all?"

"This means...I wouldn't mind getting to know more about Camden Holden."

"Call me Cam. And I want to get to know you as well."

"I like Camden, unless it bothers you?"

"No, it doesn't bother me. If you're calling me Camden that means at least you're speaking to me. Can I call you later tonight Andrea, unless you have other plans?"

She hesitated for just a moment. "That would be good."

"You do know I'll need your direct number right?"

"I know, I know. I'll email you my cell, from my personal email later today. I promise."

"I'll hold you to that, and I look forward to talking to you later."

"Me too, actually."

"Good. Have a good afternoon, *pretty eyes*."

She laughed lightly and shook her head. "Later, Camden."

Robert walked in to see Cam already half done with a beer as he sat down. Glancing at the bottle, he said, "Damn man, rough day?"

"Nope, I'm celebrating."

"You finish a project? Or you starting a new fat paying one?"

"Nope."

"We playing 'guess' today or what?"

"I'm celebrating cause you owe me $50."

"What?" Robert frowned, trying to think when he'd borrowed money from Cam, then it dawned on him. "Ahh! That woman you were digging actually contacted you huh?"

"Yeah, she emailed me today around lunch time."

"Hmm, took her a week...interesting. All you got was an email?"

Cam frowned. "I called her instead of responding back. We talked for a bit."

"You still feeling that spark?"

"I was happy she reached out, if that's what you mean."

Robert let Cam deflect. "When are you actually going to see her?"

"Not sure. Right now we've agreed to just get to know each other."

"Well, I'm rooting for you. Sounds like you have some work ahead of you."

Cam smiled and the conversation turned to their normal Friday subjects. When the waitress brought Robert his food about fifteen minutes later, she also brought a "to-go" bag for Cam.

"What's all that?"

Cam was busy pulling out some bills for a tip. "My dinner. I'm about to head out."

"Head out?" Robert glanced at his watch. "It's barely after six."

"Sorry man, I told Andrea I'd call tonight. I want to make sure I don't call too late."

"You don't want to...you blowing me off already for a woman who won't even go out with you?"

"Naw, I just don't want to be rude. Calling someone I'm just getting to know late at night, like she a booty call."

"It's cool...I see you still in denial."

"Whatever man." Cam stood up and prepared to leave. "I'll catch you later."

"Yeah, yeah. Hey, wait a minute! You sure you left enough for your food?"

"That was for a tip. I told the waitress when I first got here everything I ordered was on *you*. Take it out that fifty you owe me. You should never bet against the house." Cam started laughing as Robert scowled at him.

"Gone and run home so you can get to *caking* at a decent hour."

"I'm not caking."

"Okay, baker man, whatever you say." Robert watched Cam leave, then started eating his food.

He didn't care about his friend dipping out early. They'd both done it before, if they had a date later in the evening. What he *was* worried about was Cam being so invested in a woman he'd only met once and barely talked to. He had a feeling this was either going to end very well...or very badly.

20

Chapter Four

Cam was frustrated. It was Friday night and he was at home brooding. In the two weeks since Andrea had first contacted him, they still hadn't gone on a real date. During the first week, they kept to daily phone calls and emails. Their phone conversations were relaxed and easy, their emails fun and amusing. During the second week, they had finally met up on this Wednesday for a lunch date, and he'd made sure to arrive early so he could get a good look at her.

She was above-average height, and would come to about his shoulders with no shoes on. Her body shape was almost slim, but not quite. Luckily, the fall chill hadn't hit yet, and she walked in wearing a long-sleeved red and white striped dress that defined her hips and C-cup breasts. They alone would forever keep her from being in the slim category, which was fine with him! She had a slightly rounded face that slimmed into the prefect oval when she smiled, which she did when she caught sight of him. He noticed her hair was straight today and lightly curled. When they had met, it had been naturally curly. He didn't care which way she wore it. As long as he could get his hands in it, preferably when they were making love.

During lunch, he had learned that she liked burgers and fries, but could usually resist sweets. They'd talked about their respective work and the upcoming weekend. As they were leaving, he asked her on a date for this upcoming Friday. She had claimed she had a prior engagement with a friend. He wasn't sure he believed her, but let it go, which was easier to do when she gave him a hug as they left. The tingles dancing up and down his spine had distracted him from the goal of getting a date. By the time he'd gotten his senses back, she'd been half way down the block.

He was thoroughly enjoying getting to know her. Even things like her favorite color, which was purple, or that she didn't particularly like romance movies, which was good because he hated them. She tended to be a bit of a workaholic and preferred tea over coffee, though she was willing to drink one if she needed a boost. Now however, he was ready for more. He wanted more direct intimate contact with her, when they were not pressed for time. Cam mostly steered clear of any sexual banter, as he had the feeling she was always one step away from bolting. He wanted her badly, which was surprising considering he hadn't even kissed her yet. If he talked to her right before going to bed, it was torture. Even her voice made him want to take her on whatever flat surface she'd allow. Hell...he wasn't picky.

Running a hand over his head, he gritted his teeth. He had actually jacked off thinking of her one night. "Shit, Robert might be right. She is making me crazy." It was closing in on nine and he refused to sit in this house thinking about Andrea. Robert had a date and while he could probably tag a few other folks, he decided to head out on his own. That was the good thing about being down town in a major city, there was always something he could do or see. At a minimum there were plenty of places he could grab a stool and have a few drinks. He refused to let her dominate his thoughts tonight.

Andrea pulled on her long, thin black sweater over her knee-length blue dress. Mika had wanted a table on the patio, and since it was mid-September it could get cool at night. It had been a mild morning and afternoon, by evening not so much. Most places would probably close up their patio dining service in another week or so.

"Girl, you got me freezing out here," Andrea complained as Mika came back from the bathroom.

"It's not that bad."

"Not yet, but it will only get worse the later it gets."

"Well what did you want me to do? The wait for inside was twenty minutes. I'm starving. The appetizers we have at the meetings don't do squat. I'm going to talk with Julia about having *real* food next month."

Andrea snorted, shaking her head. "Good luck with that. You know she holds our budget strings tight. As tight as an old woman walking down the street in the dark."

Mika laughed as they both took a look at the menu. They were charter members of a nonprofit group to help mentor young African American girls, between the ages of fourteen to eighteen. They met once a month with a few other professional women and conducted different learning sessions with the girls, as well as some open talk time where they could bring up anything they wanted, either in front of the group or privately with one of the adults.

"It was a good meeting tonight," Andrea commented, putting her menu aside.

"Yeah, it was. The girls are coming along. It's Friday night though, and I want some adult conversation. What's really going on with you and your guy? I got nothing. The date I had last week was a flop. He had a foot fetish, like a *bad* one. He wanted to suck my toes. Nothing else girl. Just suck my toes on the first date. Now, I don't mind a little kink but damn!"

Andrea was still laughing, after they quickly placed their order with the waitress. "That's a shame."

"I know right. So, what is Camden into?" When Andrea just looked at her blankly, she expounded, "Sexually...what is he into sexually?"

"How would I know?"

"You've been talking to him every minute you can for over two weeks. You telling me you haven't even brought up sexual likes and dislikes, or found out something from flirting?"

"Yep, that's what I'm telling you. We talk about *real* things. Politics, current events, work, likes and dislikes."

"Exactly, likes and dislikes *in* bed."

"No, you freak."

"I'm not a freak. You're just a prude," Mika shot back.

"I'm not. We're just taking things slow. I like that about him."

"No, *you* are taking it slow. You won't even give that poor man an actual date."

"What are you talking about? We met for lunch just this week."

"Emails, calls, and one lunch, which is not a proper date, by the way. I know he's asked you out by now."

"He did, after lunch. He asked about today and I told him I had a thing with you."

"What about tomorrow?"

Andrea contritely looked away. "Umm, I told him I was busy."

"You getting on my nerves. So I *know* you have to be getting on his. Why won't you go out with him?" When her friend just shrugged, Mika continued. "What's the big deal? Did you forget how to date after six months?"

"Don't be ridiculous. It's not that." Andrea let out a sigh. "I'm a little afraid. I think I like him too much already."

Instead of sympathy Mika pressed her lips together. "Oh, boo-hoo. Andrea likes a guy, so she has to stay away from him. Girl, so far he seems normal. You better take him and be happy. Meanwhile, I'm stuck with toe suckers."

"That's part of the problem! He seems too normal, too easy going. I haven't found anything I don't like yet."

"You know what...you betta be glad service is taking forever. I'd fling a bread roll at you if I had any. Well maybe not, since I'm starving. If you don't enjoy this good, normal man while you can I will hurt you. You don't have to get deep with him, but go out give him a real chance, get out the damn house and have some fun."

"I get out the house. I have fun," Andrea said sullenly.

"Okay, fine. Then stay *in* the house and do some bed room activities. Just don't forget to share with me. I'm going through a dry spell."

Andrea just rolled her eyes and frowned. Thoughts of having Camden in her bed had kept her up at night. She should never have given him that hug. To say she had felt it down to her toes would be the exact truth. She just couldn't imagine sleeping with him, when she was half way to an orgasm from a hug. Nope, nope, nope. She should stay as far away from him as possible.

"Andrea?"

Both she and Mika looked around at the sound of her name. But she knew that voice right away. "Camden!"

"Hey, I thought that was you." Cam couldn't believe his luck. He had been walking around trying to decide where he wanted to go, when he'd caught sight of Andrea. For a moment, he'd thought he was hallucinating. He finally pulled his eyes away and gave her friend a brief smile. At least he knew she hadn't been lying about having plans with someone.

"What are you doing here?" If Andrea wore pearls, she would be clutching them. It was like her thoughts had conjured him up.

"I was just out taking in the night, since someone turned me down...I had time on my hands."

Mika finally snapped her mouth shut and spoke up. "Sorry about that. I'm the one she had plans with. Must be serendipity, as we were *just* talking about you. Why don't you join us? We just put our order in less than five minutes ago." Mika flinched as Andrea kicked her under the table.

Cam glanced at Andrea to see her glaring at her friend. He smothered a smile, as there was no way he was passing up a chance to spend time with her. "I'd love to. Let me go inside and I'll join you ladies in a moment."

Chapter Five

Andrea watched as he followed the black rail fence towards the restaurant door, then swung her head around to scowl at Mika. "Why did you do that?"

"What? It would be rude not to invite him. Besides, I'm not missing a chance to meet your sidewalk guy. Stop pouting. Get over it and enjoy. I'm here as a chaperone. No thanks needed."

"The last thing I want to do right now is thank you."

"You will my sista." Mika waved away her anger with a hand. In a lower voice, as Camden walked towards them she said, "This brother is fine! You are plain crazy not to jump on that. As long as you've been without some, you should be riding him like a pony!"

"Mika!" Andrea choked out, the imagery shocking her.

"Everything okay ladies?" Cam asked as he pulled out a chair to sit. He could actually see a blush spreading on Andrea's face.

"We're great tonight!" Mika answered, to give Andrea time to get her composure back. "I was just telling Andrea what a fine guy you seem like. That she should be taking advantage of your...your willingness to spend time with her."

"Jeez, thanks for making me sound like a charity case."

Before Mika could comment, their waitress was suddenly there, all smiles just for Camden. "Hi there! Can I get you anything to drink?"

Cam looked at the women first. "Ladies, what are we drinking tonight?"

"I could go for a glass of red wine." Mika spoke up quickly.

"What about you, Andrea?"

"I'll take a glass of red as well."

Now Cam turned his charming smile towards the waitress. "Make that three."

"Sure thing! I'll get those right to you. Do you need time before you order? Or would you like me to recommend something for you?"

"No, I'm good. Been here before." Cam placed his order and the waitress walked off, throwing him a smile over her shoulder. He noticed both women looking at each other and rolling their eyes. "What?"

"Don't tell me you didn't notice she was flirting with you," Andrea threw out, before giving Mika a look. "Mika, am I lying? We barely got water in ten minutes. He's here for about sixty seconds and is offered *recommendations*." Both women started laughing and Cam joined in.

"Hey what can I say? They have good service here."

"Yeah, if you a fine man," Mika said, not quite under her breath. Then she turned fully to Cam, leaning across the table, giving him a mischievous smile. "Now, Camden."

"Call me Cam," he interrupted.

"Cam, tell me everything about yourself."

That started the conversation off as Mika questioned him, and he good naturedly answered, or charmingly deflected when he wanted to. Andrea was impressed by how at ease he was. Most men would have gotten defensive or been uncomfortable with the whole situation. By the time their food arrived, they had moved from integration mode to regular chit chat. The wine that the waitress had rushed out was probably kicking in by then as well.

Mika had to bite her lip to keep from laughing when Andrea gave the waitress the stink eye for trying to push "dessert" on Cam. Andrea had coldly declined for the whole table and said they were ready for the bill. Mika found it hilarious! The woman was acting possessive of the man. Speaking of, the waitress was on her way back to the table.

"Here you guys go. I hope you enjoyed your meal tonight."

Andrea looked from the blonde, college-aged woman back to the single bill she'd placed in the middle of the table. "You didn't split the bill?"

"I'm sorry! I didn't think to ask again if you wanted separate checks." She quickly glanced at Camden before finishing her sentence. "Once your friend showed up-"

"No, it's not your fault." Andrea waved off the waitress distress. She seemed genuinely contrite. "We did tell you one bill we when first sat down."

"Still, I should have-"

"It's not a big deal. I got it." All three women heads snapped around to Camden as he spoke.

"I can't let you do that!" Andrea stammered out.

"You can't stop me either." He winked at her, and handed the waitress the bill along with his debit card. Mika laughed at the chagrined expression on Andrea's face, while the waitress made her escape.

"Camden, you didn't have to pay for both of us. We invited you to join us."

"It's no problem. Honest."

"Girl, the man has paid, let it go." Mika was getting a kick out of watching these two.

"But-"

"Look at it this way. I got the company of two beautiful women, a good meal and interesting conversation. Which is more than I would have gotten if I'd been somewhere by myself."

"Don't sell yourself short. I think you could have pulled off two women wherever you went."

He grinned at Mika, while Andrea threw her a dirty look.

"Don't look at me like that. He probably could! Anyway, thank you Cam for treating us tonight. I appreciate it."

He nodded his head towards Mika. "You're welcome."

Mika pointedly looked at Andrea and tapped her finger on the table. "Don't *you* have something to say to the man?"

Andrea actually wanted to smack the smirk off her best friend's face. Instead she turned an embarrassed look toward Camden. "I hate when she's both annoying and right. Thank you for the meal, that was very nice of you."

"My pleasure, pretty eyes."

Mika saw how he looked at Andrea, as if he hadn't already eaten. She shook her head slightly, thinking her friend was stupid if she didn't snatch this man up!

So she wouldn't have to watch him make sexy eyes at Andrea, she started rummaging through her purse. "Ugh, Cam, do you have any friends for me? I'd love to find a man who buys drinks and meals while giving out sweet compliments."

"Actually, I do know some-"

Mika cut him off as the waitress returned his card. "Never mind. There are rarely two good ones in a group of male friends."

Cam winced, but laughed. "Come on, that's harsh."

"No, my new friend, that's reality." Mika pulled out a twenty and threw it on the table, then gathered her purse. "I got the tip. I guess this counts as you guys first dinner date, even if you had a third wheel."

Cam grinned at her, while Andrea threw her a pained look. Ignoring her friend, she grinned back at Cam, then winked at Andrea before standing up. "I'm calling it a night, but you two kids feel free to stay out and enjoy."

Mika was waving good bye and walking away before Andrea could protest. She could actually feel it, as Camden turned his full focus on her. She grasped at something to say. "It's nice seeing you tonight, even though it wasn't planned."

Putting his hands up as a sign of innocence, he commented, "I promise it really was by chance, but I'm glad I got to spend time with you. It was nice to meet your friend too. She's funny."

Rolling her eyes, she finally smiled back at him. "Mika is a nuisance, is what she is. Are you sure she didn't put you up to coming here tonight? I wouldn't put it past her to have stolen my phone at some point and texted you a time and place."

"Wow, no she didn't. But...if she had, I would have come, no questions asked, thinking the request came from you." He reached out and put his hand on hers, mingling their fingers on top of the table. Like always, electricity seemed to pass between them.

"Be careful Cam, that sounds like I have you wrapped around my little finger."

He turned her palm over and ran his finger tip down the middle of it, making her draw in a breath. He looked up into her eyes with a serious and intent expression on his face. "Not yet, but I have a feeling it wouldn't take much."

Slowly, she withdrew her hand, giving him a shy smile. She wasn't rejecting him, she just needed a little distance as she processed his words. "Well then, you should be very cautious around me."

Now he sat back in his chair grinning playfully. "Where would be the fun in that? Speaking of...let's get out here and do something." Saying so he stood up and held out his hand. "You game?"

She hesitated for just a second before placing her hand in his. "I'm game, Mr. Holden."

Chapter Six

As they walked away from the restaurant, he put his arm through hers, pulling her near his side. She didn't mind, as his warmth felt good against the chilly air. She squeezed his arm briefly to get his attention and looked up at him. "I want to you know I'm glad you joined us tonight. I know I may have seemed bothered when you first showed up, but I was honestly surprised to see you."

"No, I get it. You had plans with your girl and here I come out the blue intruding."

"You were fine, seriously. Mika and I mentor a group of young girls once a month. We had just finished up our meeting and were grabbing something to eat. You weren't interrupting anything. I see her all the time anyway."

"Ahh, so you saying you would rather be with me?"

She grinned at his infectious smile before shaking her head. "I'm *saying* I was glad to see you, even though I wasn't expecting to. Don't let it go to your head."

"I don't think I've had that problem, since dealing with you." She gave him a small nudge with her shoulder and he laughed, pulling her back close. "How much further is your car?

"Just up there in the next lot. So, where are we going? It's almost 10:30."

"How about TV Lounge? They usually have a good mix of music, and I'm really interested to see your moves."

"I like that place!"

"Good, but you'll have to drive."

"I can do that. How far away did you park?"

"Remember I told you I don't live far from downtown. Sometimes I walk, then take a bus the rest of the way. I did that tonight, as I wasn't expecting to have company. I just wanted to get out the house so I could stop thinking about a certain someone named Andrea."

She stopped them a few feet before the lot entrance and faced him. "That's laying it on a bit thick don't you think?" She was calling him out on the game he was trying to run.

"Not at all. I have no reason to lie or embellish. That was just a statement of fact. You stay on my mind...a lot."

Andrea was totally perplexed as she saw he was one hundred percent serious. She'd never dealt with men who were comfortable being so honest with their feelings. Most made a point of pretending not to care one way or the other about a woman until they were heavy into a relationship. She didn't know how to feel knowing that he was apparently thinking about her as much as she was him. To top it off, now she felt like an idiot.

"Hmm, okay. My car is right there." She walked ahead of him, giving a little wave to the attendant who was smirking at her and Camden. He was probably noticing she'd left the car alone, yet came back with a man. She lengthened her stride, rolling her eyes at the same time. Why the hell did she care what some stranger thought of her in the first place?

Reaching the car she popped the locks and suddenly found Camden there, opening her door. "Oh, thanks." That was another thing that always threw her off about him. He was only thirty, yet he actually had manners. Some would say even old fashioned ones. Yet he was definitely easy going and playful as well. As he got into the car and they buckled up, she asked him about it. "You have the manners of someone twice your age."

He raised an eyebrow at her statement and got comfortable in the car. "How would you know? You date a lot of sixty year olds?"

"No!" The preposterous question made her laugh. "I'm just saying. You said you grew up here, and no offense, but I haven't met that many men from this area that are as mannerly as you."

"Aww, come on. Though I'll admit, I picked up a lot of what I know from when I was at school down south."

"Duke right?"

"Yeah, you know with all the southern belles."

"Okay, okay, I get it. Well, I guess I should be happy I get to reap the rewards."

"That's a good way to look at it." They chatted for the ten minutes it took to get to the club until he said, "See if you can get that spot on the street." He pointed it out and she was able to edge out a car coming from the other direction.

"Can't believe we got that spot. It's early, but it seems pretty packed."

"I think we got lucky is all. It puts us right at the door," Cam said, before getting out.

She took the time to figure out if she wanted to leave her sweater in the car. She opted to do so since they were so close to the entrance. Once inside, Camden paid the cover charge and lead her to the bar. They got lucky again, grabbing two open bar seats. Instead of sitting, she leaned over to him and shouted over the salsa music, "Let me run to the restroom, I'll be right back."

"I'll get some drinks. What do you want?"

"Get me an amaretto sour."

"Done."

She walked off, dodging in and out of the crowd to reach the bathroom. Quickly doing her business, she washed her hands and freshened up her lipstick. She was starting to feel nervous, as well as excited. It had been at least four months since she went out dancing with a group of girlfriends. She loved to dance, but didn't get to do it often, much less with a man. Now she would be dancing with Camden, a man who could get her hot and bothered, with a look. Just the thought made her want to run…but she wasn't sure if she would be running *away* from him, or *towards* him.

"Get a grip," she muttered to herself before smoothing down her dress and walking back out into the crowd.

The back of Cam's neck tingled, and turning he saw her a few steps away. What was it about her that made him so aware of her presence? He finally had her alone and he planned to soak up every moment. "Just in time," he told her. "Drinks just arrived."

They consumed their drinks at the bar watching others on the dance floor, laughing and talking in between. They brushed up against each other as they got close to talk. Several times, his plump lips lightly grazed her earlobe, sending prickles of heat down her spine. She was enjoying his company and the music. She hadn't realized how much she needed, *wanted* to relax. Now, she was ready to do more than just tap her feet. Taking a big swallow to finish her drink, she gave him a saucy grin before standing up.

"Okay, I'm ready to dance!" This time, she was the one to hold out a hand to him.

He took it, bringing her knuckles up for a kiss. "If you're ready, I'm ready."

"That's What I Like" by Bruno Mars was on when they hit the floor. It was prefect to get them dancing, as they flowed into the rhythm of the song and the jostling of the crowd. The DJ played a few more pop songs, then switched to rap. That's why she loved this place, they mixed it up and she liked a lot of different music. They stayed out on the floor, dancing to it all.

Cam was loving it. Ms. *Cool* Cole, could move. She had on a work appropriate dress, or at least it would be if she had that sweater over it. Without it, the dress hugged her body and more than showed off every curve. He got to see her lose herself in the music. She was definitely not shy while dancing, which led him to believe she wouldn't be in the bedroom either. He was more determined than ever that he'd eventually end up in her bed. Twirling her around, he saw her point to her throat, then the bar.

Pulling her under his arm, Cam started maneuvering them back to the bar. He liked having her close, letting everyone know she was with him. It was an odd thought to have, and *felt* even odder. He'd honestly never thought about stuff like this while out with other women. He had already stared down several men tonight, whose eyes lingered on her body longer then he appreciated. Thinking about it, he could honestly say he'd never minded if men showed his dates some attention from afar. If he was being real, he hadn't even minded knowing other men *wanted* the woman he was with. But now...he didn't even want anyone else *thinking* about Andrea.

The revelation made him stop in his tracks, causing her to look up at him in question. Moving forward again, he squeezed them in at the bar. The crowd had swelled, and it was standing room only.

"You want some water or a drink?"

"Both," Andrea replied as Camden caught the eye of a bartender. It was a woman who smiled a little too broadly as she made her way over. Andrea found herself automatically scooting closer to Camden.

"Got it." He ordered two waters and turned back to her. "What you want to drink?"

"A whiskey sour this time."

"Okay, I see you upgrading." She just laughed as he turned back to the bar. "A whiskey sour, and I'll take a whiskey neat, to match my lady."

As the server went to make their drinks, Andrea felt a little flutter in her stomach. "I'm your lady now am I?"

Leaning back, he brushed her collarbone lightly, looking at her seriously for a moment before smirking and leaning forward. "Yeah, that's right, you just haven't realized it yet."

"Did you know you can be cocky?" When he just shrugged, she continued, "I'll admit it can be sexy at times."

"Good to know. I'll keep that in mind."

When the drinks arrived, they took their time, watching the floor again. Eventually, they went back out when some slow songs started playing. They swayed against each other, and Andrea didn't know if it was the drinks or the music or just him, but she was feeling slightly dizzy. He felt *so* good. Her first impression of him on that sidewalk had been correct. He was built very solidly. The closest she could get to describing his body type was athletic. She bet if his shirt was off, he'd look like a basketball player. She knew he was only mildly into sports, so she wondered how he kept his body in such good shape. Maybe he worked out a lot? That thought put the image of him weight lifting in her mind, his chest straining and glistening with sweat.

She needed to stop! Luckily, a slightly more up-tempo song came on and she was glad for a minute until she figured out it was "Wild Thoughts". The devil was out to get her! She loved this song and the lyrics seemed appropriate as she was having wild, sexy thoughts about Camden. Thoughts that she knew were dangerous to be having about this man. Even so, she started moving her body in ways that matched the sensual tone embodied in the lyrics.

38

Cam had to blink a couple of times to make sure he was seeing this right. He sure was *feeling it*. As she backed that ass up on him just long enough for his eyes to get a little crossed, before turning to face him again. Swiveling her hips slowly from side to side, while sliding her hands slowly down from his neck to his chest. Apparently, his body had no problem keeping up, as he matched her vibe.

Then their eyes connected, and it was like the rest of the room disappeared. Suddenly they were in a world of their own. They moved as one, their hands outright caressing each other as they went. She danced like a video vixen, to the words and beat meant to entice a man. Well, Cam was fully seduced and if he'd been paying attention he would have noticed a number of other men were as well. They were probably being obscene, but he didn't give a damn. When the song ended, they were pressed chest-to-chest, his hands holding her firmly by the top swells of her lush behind. It wasn't until a man who was a few feet away called out, "Damn, your girl is hot!" that they became aware of their surroundings again.

Camden didn't shoot his normal disarming smile her way. Instead, he was looking at her in a way that had her trying to take a step back. He tightened his grip before finally letting go. She took his hand lightly and led him away from the floor.

"Hey, what time is it?"

Cam pulled his phone from his back pocket and checked. "About one o'clock."

"Time went fast, but I think I'm ready to call it a night." He nodded and she continued. "Let me hit the restroom, since I have a bit of a drive home." Living in Dearborn, she really didn't have that far to go, but at the moment she'd take any excuse to put a little space between them. Besides, the second drink and water had caught up with her.

He nodded again, pointing to the entrance. "I'll wait for you by the door."

Coming out the stall, she looked at herself in the mirror. Had she really been the woman out on that dance floor, pretending to be Rihanna? Her body was still heated, her heart was still beating too fast…all from one dance.

"Shit," she muttered, then washed her hands, freshened up her lipstick, and popped a few breath mints. She decided to check her phone as she stalled for more time. She ignored the couple of texts from Mika, not even reading them. Putting the phone back in her purse, she gave herself a lecture.

Andrea Cole, you are going to drop him off, say goodnight and go straight home! No passing go into his house. Don't even hug him. He doesn't even get a handshake. Touching that man is dangerous.

Hoping that was enough to guide her in the right direction, she squared her shoulders, pasted on a small smile, and went out to find Camden.

Chapter Seven

The drive to his house was strained. Camden wasn't his playful self. He gave her brief, distracted directions while she drove. There was definitely tension inside the car. She didn't make it any better as she turned on the music and didn't try to engage in conversation either. She'd put her sweater back on before leaving, remarking it was chilly. If only her cooling skin could suppress the inner heat in her belly. Her body was anticipating something that her brain was determined not to let happen.

Camden was too busy trying to get himself under control to pretend that the sizzle they'd felt at the club never happened. Hell, he didn't *want* to pretend. What he wanted was to make her pull this car over and take her in the front seat. He was envisioning pulling her over the middle console, hiking her dress up over those full hips, and pushing his hard cock into her waiting warmth. She could ride him til they both came! After all, she'd just showed him that she had rhythm. He shifted in the seat to keep from adjusting what was in his pants, and focused on telling her the last few turns to his house.

The drive had taken about fifteen minutes, and he'd spent the whole time thinking about what his next move should be. Should he press the sexual connection from the club or ease off? He was *trying* to think with his brain instead of his dick. He could see she was nervous and would prefer to ignore the chemistry that had sparked into flames tonight. She'd come back from the bathroom cool enough, acting undisturbed by their display on the dance floor. He could tell she was trying to put the genie back in the bottle, but he wasn't sure if he was going to let that happen.

"Turn right at this next street, and I'm the first house on the corner to your left."

"Okay, got it." Andrea's hands tensed on the steering wheel as she took a right and then pulled up to the brown brick house. It was dark, but she could see from the flood lights that he kept up his yard and the outside of the house. Not that any of it was holding her attention right now. Should she leave the car running or would that be overreacting a bit? She pulled up a little more before turning off the ignition. "Well, here you go. From what I can see, you have a very nice house."

"Thanks."

His short response had her looking in his direction. She turned in her seat to face him. "I had a really good time tonight Camden. Thank you again for dinner and dancing."

He reached out to caress the side of her face, while using the other hand to unbuckle his seat belt. "Thank you for allowing me to spend time with you."

Was it just her, or was his voice a couple of octaves lower? And why was she turning her face into his palm? "It's late...I should be going," Andrea stuttered out.

"Yes, you should." No one moved. Cam watched as she lowered her eyes and bit her lip, and that was it for him. He surged forward, grabbing the other side of her face, before kissing her. She opened for him like his lips were a key to a lock. His tongue swept in, tasting whiskey and mints. As far as he was concerned, at this moment it was the best taste on Earth.

Andrea melted as soon as his lips met hers. Any rational thought left her, and it was all she could do to stay upright. She clutched at his shoulder and waist just to steady herself, as the onslaught to her mouth continued. Lord, this was bad...so bad and *so* good! When his tongue stroked the roof of her mouth she shivered, before sucking on his tongue in retaliation.

Cam felt the pull low in his belly and it drove him a little wild! He tried to yank her closer only to be hindered by her seatbelt. With a growl of impatience, he released it. Then in a show of strength, heightened by arousal, he pulled her across the car into his lap.

She had a few seconds to breathe before his lips were back on hers. Her mind trying to process having her ass sitting firmly on top of his manhood, her back almost against his door. The only thing she truly understood, was that if he sexily growled at her again, she was liable to do anything he wanted.

Part of his mind was telling him to slow down. Of course he ignored it, and took advantage of the access this new position afforded him, snaking his hand up to her breast. He heard her moan and continued to gently squeeze before purposely running his palm over her extended nipple. He felt it as she inhaled sharply, so he did it again and again before pressing the nipple between his fingers. She gave another throaty moan, and he glided his hand down to her knees before starting his ascent.

Andrea was wishing she had worn a less conservative dress, something with some give so he could bare her breast. She broke the deep kiss, and gave him kisses along his jaw and chin. She delighted in his heavy breathing, but not as much as she delighted in his hand slowly moving up between her thighs, pushing her dress out the way as he went. Delighted or not, she probably should put a halt to this madness! When he squeezed her upper thigh, her legs parted of their own accord. At the first stroke of his finger over the middle of her panties, her brief stint with rational thought was over.

By the second stroke, he found her lips again and was kissing her greedily, even though his finger kept a slow tempo. She clutched at his neck while his hands drove her crazy. Before long, she wanted him to move faster, to put more pressure right where she needed it, but he refused. Instead, he kept the pace frustratingly slow. Her hips begin to move, trying to give her what his fingers denied.

Cam knew she wanted more, he could hear it in her sighs and moans, feel it as her hands grew clingier. He understood the feeling, he was holding on by a thread himself! He could feel the wetness awaiting him through her panties and wanted so badly to sink into it. Cam however, had the long game in mind, not just short-term rewards. He wanted her as hot as he was. He finally sped up his hand and heard the skip in her breath. He broke the kiss to watch her face, gritting his own teeth. The more she squirmed around in his lap, the more he thought he might burst and embarrass himself. He heard the cadence of her breathing change and increased the pressure he was putting on her clit with each stroke.

Andrea's head fell back so quickly that she could hear the small thump it made against the passenger side window. She couldn't care less if she had a concussion, as long as he didn't stop. This was crazy! She was close to climaxing! Right now, there was nothing more important than reaching that goal. She moved her hips again asking for more...and this time he gave it to her.

Cam was breathing almost as hard as she was, as he leaned forward to suck along her exposed neck, his finger alternating now between hard strokes and circles. He wanted nothing more than to sink his fingers in her hot heat and feel her cum. He still held off, even as her body started to tense...and then he stopped. He saw her eyes immediately open, saw the quick look of confusion and just as quickly, saw it flicker to annoyance.

"Why did you stop? I was *so* clo-"

He cut her off, squeezing her thigh to get her attention. "Do you still think you should go?" He whispered the question in her ear before drawing back so he could see her face. Her passion-filled eyes cleared enough to understand what he was really asking.

Andrea's brain struggled to catch up. One second, she was on the verge of cumming, and the next he was asking her to think...to decide what their next steps would be. Vaguely, she recognized she should be glad he was giving her a chance to reconsider, but right now she just wanted what he'd been *so close* to giving her. She shook her head in an attempt to clear it, sitting up as much as she could. Looking in those caramel eyes that had first caught her attention she answered.

"Would it be okay...if I come in?"

"Hell yes!"

Camden didn't waste any time maneuvering her out of the car on his side. Before she could overthink it, he grabbed her purse from the back and took the keys out the ignition. He shut the door, activated the alarm, then handed her the keys and bag. He was wrapping his arm around her waist and walking them to the door in twelve seconds flat.

His hands were actually trembling a bit. It felt like he'd been waiting for this moment forever. He'd gone from not being able to get her on a simple date to having her in his house, ready for sex. He didn't know how the hell they'd gone from zero to a hundred, but he didn't plan on blowing his chance. He was going to make sure she didn't regret her choice tonight. With that in mind, he figured he'd better slow things down. As he shut and locked the door, he saw her looking around. He had left a few lights on throughout the house, since he figured he would get in late.

Andrea placed her purse on the living room table, her head still spinning with the decision she'd made. She was really in his house...this was going to happen. It may have seemed as if she was looking at the house, but in reality she didn't see anything. She'd expected to be pounced on as soon as they cleared the door, but he still stood a few feet away, hungrily watching her.

"Do you want something to eat...drink?"

She smiled hesitantly at him and walked the few feet towards him. "What I'd like, is to go to your bedroom and finish what we started in the car." She figured in for a penny, in for a pound...right? She saw his eyes flash with surprise before he grabbed her hand and tugged her toward the stairs.

"What the lady wants...the lady is about to get."

Camden led her up to his darkened bedroom, turning up the dimmer switch until the room was lit up enough for him to see clearly. He was not going to miss seeing every inch of this woman. He closed the door with his foot, and when she turned to him with a shy smile, he gathered her in his arms. While he tried to kiss her senseless again, he also dealt with her sweater, before sliding his hands to her ass.

He was happy to see her hands were just as busy as his, sliding his blazer off his shoulders. When she moved to his belt, his allowed his jacket to slide to the floor before he unzipped the back of her dress. He unhooked her bra and pulled it down along with the dress until he'd exposed her breasts. He couldn't resist tasting them for another moment. Dipping his head down, he slowly drew her flesh into his mouth.

Andrea responded by arching her back and standing on her toes so that he could take more. She put a hand under his shirt and ran them up his firm chest. Placing a palm over his heart, she was gratified to feel the quick, hard beat of it. He was taking strong pulls of her flesh, and to show her appreciation, she flicked her nails over his nipple.

Cam backed up for a brief moment to rid himself of his shirt so that her hands could roam more freely. Andrea took the time to finish tugging her dress down and off. He came back and took her other breast while his hand caressed its twin. Attacking his pants again, Andrea wanted him to be just as naked as she was. She finally got the damn belt off. Unzipping him, she was finally able to reach her hand inside to get her first feel of what would soon be inside her.

Even inside his underwear she could tell he was wide and long. He stepped out of his pants and kicked them aside as his lips traveled up her neck to take her mouth again. He kissed her passionately until he felt her knees go weak, then took the opportunity to move her backwards a few steps closer to the bed. Tumbling her onto the mattress, he slid her damp panties down her shapely hips. She scooted backwards to pull her body fully on the bed and Cam followed, crawling between her legs. He wedged his shoulders against her thighs, spreading her wide for his consumption.

He started with kisses, nips, then licks to soothe the sting along each side of her thighs, making her both jump and shiver. Andrea raised her head and shoulders and said on a shaky exhale, "You don't have to..."

He glanced up and caught her eye, giving her the most intense, predatory stare she had ever gotten from a man in her life.

"I not only *want* to...I've had several dreams of doing this."

She nodded weakly in consent and let her head fall back. *Jeezus!* Who was she to deny a man his dream?

Camden didn't start slow, instead he plunged his tongue deep inside her, savoring the warm rich taste of her. He retreated to take a slow lick up either side of her clit, before finally sucking gently on the bud. He licked from her opening back up before swirling the nub with his tongue. Cam repeated variations of the process, alternating sequence and rhythm. When her breathing began to catch, he inserted two fingers and began to move them firmly within her.

That elicited a drawn-out moan from her throat. "Cam...yes!" He refocused his mouth where it was needed the most, flicking and tonguing her with abandon, which soon had her cumming around his fingers and arching up from the bed. Andrea was still riding the high of her climax, so she didn't notice Cam hurriedly removing his last piece of clothing until he slid his body alongside hers.

She instantly wrapped her legs and arms around him. Luxuriating in the feel of them being skin-to-skin, not a shred of clothing between them. She could feel his enlarged penis on her stomach and hip, as he reached over to open his bedside drawer. She heard the crinkle of a condom and her thighs clenched in anticipation. When he sat up to sheath himself, she rained kisses on his neck and chest, even sliding down a bit to lick his nipples while her hands roamed his back.

Cam caught his fingers in her hair and pulled her head back for a ferocious kiss. He was hard as a rock and had no desire to hold back. Disentangling from her limbs, he flipped her on her stomach and she eagerly raised herself into position. Loving the feel of his hands stroking down her back, her hips, and then her buttocks as he parted her thighs. She moistened her lips, hungry for what was to come.

He eased into her with one sure and steady thrust. They both let out groans of pleasure at finally being joined. Giving himself only a few seconds to appreciate the tight, hot feel of her around him, he begin to thrust in earnest. It didn't take long before they both became more frenzied. He slammed into her as she reared back to meet him, taking every inch he had to offer.

She arched her back downward so he could go deeper. He started hitting a spot inside her that made her feel like she was eating the sweetest strawberry! It felt so good she clutched at the bed, biting her lip though it didn't stop her cries of satisfaction from escaping. Her breathing became shorter, more unsteady, and she was nearing another peak, when he reached around her and lightly rubbed her clit. That was all it took and she shattered, crying out, *"Cam!"* Her body was still shaking as he pulled out and gave her left butt-cheek a sharp smack.

"It's not over yet baby, not yet." He gently turned her onto her back and eased between her lax legs once more. Cam grunted as he felt the aftershocks still flowing through her as he entered. He was hanging on by a thin thread, but he wanted to look at her face when he came.

Andrea felt him begin to move within her, this time slower, his strokes long and deep. She opened her eyes and saw him watching her single-mindedly. The surface of his brow was dotted with sweat. His lips parted as he breathed hard to take in oxygen for his straining muscles. She felt her body start to respond again and her eyes went wide. She was on the verge of her third orgasm. She didn't know if she could take it. The fire inside her started as embers, but quickly caught hold and morphed into a flame. She let her hands roam to any piece of his skin she could reach. She loved seeing his eyes start to lose focus. His thrusts become harder. She loved it! She angled up to take his lips in a kiss.

As their tongues struggled, both of their releases climbed nearer as their bodies strained to reach their goal. He shifted his weight to pin her down, pushing her legs up towards her chest as his climax neared. His strokes became jerky, his arms began to shake, as his balls tightened. When her hoarse voice uttered out his name as she quivered and clenched around him, he finally let himself cum, jerking against her, once, twice, three times, before collapsing on top of her.

Chapter Eight

The wonderful weight of *man* went to lift off her body, only for her legs to hug him close. She felt a kiss on her collarbone, and heard his low chuckle before he pulled away and the bed shifted. When she heard the creak of the bedroom door, she opened her eyes, staring at the ceiling. Feeling the sting at the back of her eyes, she squeezed them tight. There would be no irrational tears. Pushing curly hair off her face, she took a few deep breaths. This was moving too fast, whatever *this* was. My god! She hadn't had sex this good, well *ever*. Body parts not used in a very long time were still tingling, still humming. The way he made her feel should be outlawed. Already, she could feel herself longing for more.

She was usually a one-and-done kind of girl, which had annoyed the men she'd dated in the past. The fact that she'd climaxed multiple times was unheard of. When had that ever happened without a vibrator? She was feeling way in over her head, one hundred percent overwhelmed. What was she supposed to do with a virtual stranger who made her body sing like this?

With a grunt of effort, she propped herself up on her elbows just as Camden walked back in, naked as the day he was born. Though surely, not as magnificently formed. She couldn't stop her eyes from moving over him, only to find herself mortified at her frank appraisal before turning her head away.

"You like what you see, huh?" Cam asked, amused by her shyness, although not surprised.

"You could pretend not to notice me looking."

"Why would I want to do that? I like that *you like* what you see." Walking over to the dresser, Cam pulled out a t-shirt before handing it to her.

"I never *said* I liked it." Andrea looked at the t-shirt that would surely be too big on her, but it was better than having a conversation naked, so she pulled it on.

Cam sat on the bed and waited until her head popped out of the shirt, catching her eye before he replied, "You liked it." He leaned in and gave her a slow kiss.

Andrea groaned and reluctantly moved away. "Bathroom?" She murmured, before turning away to get out of bed.

"Down the hall to your left, I left the light on for you. Let me know if you need anything."

Andrea escaped to the bathroom as quickly as her shaky legs would allow. She used the facilities and freshened up with the towels he'd thoughtfully left out for her, ignoring the twinges of discomfort, as she had more pressing problems. For the third time tonight, she was lecturing herself in a bathroom mirror.

"Okay, you can do this. So what? You had sex....*great* sex....*fantastic* sex, that doesn't mean anything. Go back in there and just be an adult. Consenting adults sleep with each other all the time. Don't be weird about it."

She put her chin up proudly, intending to march back into the bedroom, but those pesky sore muscles she had ignored put a stop to that plan. Instead, she gingerly made her way back to the room. She found him dressed thankfully, in a pair of navy boxers stretched out in bed. When he noticed her, all her composure fled.

Cam saw her hand nervously playing with the end of his t-shirt. He liked having something of his on her, though he'd prefer her naked again. His grin grew as he imagined how he planned to coax her back to bare skin. Then he noticed her walking towards her clothes on the floor instead of back to bed.

"This was nice, but I should be going. I have to get up early tomorrow and you know..." Andrea babbled as she bent down to pick up her dress, bra, and sweater. When she only saw one of her shoes, and had no clue where her panties were, she started to panic. "This was great, I just-"

"Hey, what's going on here?" He asked, coming off the bed, utterly confused.

"Nothing...I'm just...I don't see my other shoe and I need to leave."

Taking hold of her wrists, he asked, "Baby, what's wrong?" She looked up at him with thinly veiled panic in her eyes, so he asked again. "What's wrong? Talk to me." He shook her clothing loose from her hands and led her over to sit on the edge of the bed.

Andrea wanted to sink through the floor at her idiotic behavior. Instead, she pulled it together and did what she should have done from the start, used her words like a grown-ass woman. Words were her livelihood for goodness sake! She was the one who acknowledged a problem, assessed it, formulated solutions for it, and then had to convince bull-headed men that her ideas were valid. There was no reason she couldn't do the same in this situation. Scooting out of his arms, because she needed the physical distance, she addressed the worried man at her side.

"I'm *so* sorry that I freaked out on you. You did nothing to deserve that."

"It's okay. I just want to make sure you're all right."

"I'm fine...that's not quite true." Breathing deeply, she continued. "I want to say up front that I enjoyed everything that we did together tonight. *Everything*. I was right there with you, every step of the way. The sex we just had was frankly amazing for me."

His shoulders relaxed a bit, and he gave her a small smile. "That's a good thing, right?"

"It would be, if I wasn't me." Frowning, she reached out to hold his hand. "I don't normally move so fast when it comes to taking a relationship to a physical level. No, let me rephrase. I've never *had* such an intense physical reaction to a man so quickly. We barely know each other."

"I had no clue the evening would end like this either. Trust me, this was only in my wildest dreams."

"I believe you. I just think it would be better if I went home."

"I don't understand. We just established this is uncharted sexual territory for both of us, but that's no reason for you to leave." He reached up to palm her face and just like in the car, she found herself automatically leaning into it. "Why can't we have fun figuring it out together?"

He kissed her slowly, but it didn't take long for the intensity to build for both of them. When he grabbed the back of her neck and started to lean her backwards, Andrea broke away and pushed at his chest.

"Now see, this is why I have to leave. If I stay, you'll want to be together again. Hell, I will too. I don't know how you'll take this, and I'll actually understand if you're upset, but this is too much for me. I want...I'd like to back it up some."

"You want to back it up?" Cam ran a hand over his head. "What exactly does that mean? Spell it out for me."

"I want to still talk to you, see you, spend time with you like tonight." She flushed and hurried on. "I mean tonight *before* we had sex. I want to continue to date and get to know you. I know it's a lot to ask...taking the sex out *after* the fact, but that's where I'm at right now."

Cam was quiet as he tried to comprehend what she was asking for. Hell and bells! Did she understand what she was asking him to do? It was hard enough not going crazy thinking about her when he *hadn't* known what she felt like, looked like, and tasted like. He was getting hard again just thinking about it. This was like asking a crackhead to magically forget the pipe.

This time, he rubbed his hand down his face before focusing back on her. What he saw was a woman whose lips were still swollen from their kisses, who had love bites on her neck and upper chest. Her eyes were already resigned, even though he hadn't said a word yet. If she only knew how confused he was feeling. One thing he *did* know was that he wasn't going to back away. Yeah, fuck that. If she'd wanted to get rid of him, she should have never let him taste the sweetness between her thick thighs. Before she could speak, he held up a hand and asked, "So, let me get this straight. You'll let me take you out on legit dates?"

"Yes."

"We'll continue to call, text, and email like we've been doing?"

"Absolutely."

"But you don't want to have sex again?

Now she hesitated. "Yes, that's what I'm saying."

"For how long?"

"Well...I don't know." She threw her hands up in frustration. "I swear I'm not one of those women who count the days or go by some stupid ninety-day rule. It could be a couple of weeks or a couple of months. I honestly don't know when I'll be comfortable..." She waved at the bed. "Doing this again."

He grew silent. Assessing and thinking, before he finally said, "Okay."

"Okay?" Was she hearing him right?

"Yeah. No sex until you do what you did tonight and explicitly ask me for it."

"You're okay with this?"

"Let's say I can live with it...for as long as you can. *However*, everything outside of sex is on the table though."

"Meaning?" It was Andrea's turn for clarity.

"Meaning, we'll cuddle...you women like that right? We'll fool around when the mood hits both of us. Just like you wanted, taking it back, but *not* back to square one. We'll be two folks dating...hoping to eventually have sex with each other."

Andrea searched his face, looking for the catch but he seemed to be serious and sincere. "That...works for me."

"Good!" He gave her one of his playful smiles. "That's settled. Now, let's get some sleep. The last sex I may ever have with you, wore me out."

"I...still think I should go home." After all when he smiled at her like that, she wanted to drop her drawers, not that she had any on. At this rate, she'd be asking him to take her before the sun rose.

"Andrea, it's well past two in the morning. I'd worry about you driving home this late. We're two tired adults, we can share a bed and get some sleep."

She hesitated, but then all at once, the adrenaline her panic attack had afforded her evaporated and left her feeling tired and achy. She trusted the man in front of her with her physical safety. It was her mental state that she always worried about with him. "You are absolutely right Camden, I'll stay."

"I liked it better when you were calling me Cam," he said huskily.

This surprised a laugh out of her, and she pushed him off the bed. "Whatever, *Camden*. Why don't you get the lights? Which side of the bed do you normally sleep on?"

Cam scooped up their clothing, still littered on the floor and tossed them on a chair in the corner before moving to the light switch. "It doesn't matter. I'll take whatever side is next to you."

"You are incorrigible!"

Andrea couldn't believe how happy she felt right now, as the room blinked into darkness. He hadn't turned her away or lashed out at her for wanting to slow things down. She finally scooted under the light summer bedcover, and soon after felt his weight on the mattress. He got close enough to drape an arm around her waist from behind, but not so close that his full body was touching hers. She relaxed, and sighing with contentment, was asleep before her brain could think of much else.

Chapter Nine

She didn't wake up in the same position that she had fallen asleep in. Camden was wrapped around her better than any blanket, and the warmth of him felt delicious. As the fog of sleep cleared, she wondered how he would handle the morning hard-on currently pressing into her back. She could think of a few things she'd like to do with it. She tried to scoot away and heard him shift. She shook his arm to wake him before trying to move away again.

"Camden? Let go." She heard him grumble and finally felt him loosen his grip. She scooted up in bed as he finally opened his eyes.

"Good morning, Ms. Cole."

"Morning." Did his morning voice have to be sexy as hell too?

"What time is it?"

She looked at the bedside clock. "Umm, about ten minutes to ten."

"Good, we still got time to go to the Coney. They serve breakfast up to eleven." Cam turned away from her to roll out of bed. He couldn't look at her for long or he might make a grab for her.

"I don't need breakfast. I can just head home."

"Not this again. Look, I'm taking you to breakfast before you leave. You can grab a quick shower in the bathroom up here. I'll use the one downstairs. Towels are in the hall closet. There's probably even an extra toothbrush in there if you want it. You gone need something for your hair, or what?"

Andrea closed her mouth at his high-handed orders and put a hand in her hair. "Umm...no, as long as you have an adjustable shower head, I should be fine."

"Good. Try not to take too long. We don't want to miss the cut-off."

He was gone out the door before she could think of anything else to say. She was a little miffed at him ordering her around, but then again, she *was* hungry and she'd promised the man she'd act normal and let him take her out on dates. Honestly, she'd expected his tune to change with the light of day. She had been prepared for him to get rid of her as fast as he could. Then of course, the calls and emails would eventually dry up and she'd never hear from him again. Instead, it seemed like he meant his words from last night. He actually wanted to continue their fledgling relationship. That made a little spot in her chest feel tight.

After using the bathroom, she took a ten-minute shower, more to soothe her muscles than anything else. She brushed her teeth and left her hair to worry about after she got dressed. Going back into the bedroom, she found her clothes laid neatly out on the bed, her purse from downstairs was there as well. He'd even managed to find her other shoe and panties, bless his heart. He was being thoughtful again, as apparently was his way. She sighed, put on her clothes, and found a couple of bobby pins in her purse to put her hair in mild order. She finished with some lipstick, and felt more in control. Picking up her purse, she went downstairs to start this new chapter in their relationship.

She had won the argument to drive herself to the Coney a couple of miles away, where they'd had a surprisingly relaxed breakfast. They had parted ways close to noon with a hug, a brief kiss and a promise from him to call her tomorrow. Right now, she was too tired and full of food to let her neurosis about would he call take over. She just wanted her bed! Coming through her back door, she kicked off her shoes, locked up, grabbed her phone and immediately went to her bedroom.

Not all her aches were from the glorious sex she'd had. Some were from all that dancing in heels. It was another reminder that she wasn't as young as she used to be...or that she needed to work out more. Probably both. Undressing quickly she threw on a nightshirt and flopped flat on the bed. Rolling over, she went to set an alarm on her phone for three in the afternoon, when she noticed the five texts from Mika. She went back and opened up the first from last night.

> *Mika: What ya'll doing? You didn't run away yet did you?*
> *Mika: You better not blow it. He is fine, funny and nice...and fine!*
> Mika: Oh so you just gone ignore me after I hooked you up? You petty

Chuckling after reading the ones from last night she moved to the two from this morning.

> *Mika: OMG did he kidnap you? You betta be tied up somewhere...against your will...to not be answering me*
> *Mika: I'm legit worried, you don't even know him that well! If you breathing you better respond before I call the police on his fine ass*

Andrea sat up in bed, as Mika had sent that one only thirty minutes ago. Wanting to laugh yet touched by the concern, she rushed to text back.

> *Andrea: So now you concerned that I don't know him that well? Didn't stop you from leaving me alone with him last night did it?*

Mika: Heffa you alive! Call me!
Andrea: No

As she expected, her phone rang ten seconds later. She sent it to voicemail and got under the covers, only to get another text.

Mika: Just so you know, I'm gone hurt you next time I
see you
Andrea: I'll call you tomorrow promise
Mika: Kay...I want thesis level details when you do bye

Grinning, Andrea tossed her phone aside and welcomed sleep.

Refreshed by the time she woke up on Sunday morning, she tackled the chores she'd been too lazy to do on Saturday. Between loads of laundry, she'd called her parents as per her usual routine, reminding them she was excited about seeing them in a few months for Christmas. They were a small, but close-knit family, as she was an only child. She loved them and even though they only lived five hours away in Cincinnati, she didn't visit that often. She was living her life and they were living theirs. She saw them an average of four or five times a year, which wasn't that bad. They had been empty nesters for a decade and in the last few years, had started pestering her about when the grandkids were coming.

Surprisingly it was mostly from her dad! She had a suspicion he worried about her being alone without a man more than he was jonesing for a grandchild. Thankfully, they were not too annoying with the "when are you getting a man and settling down" routine, but it was brought up each time she went home. She wondered if she would have anything to tell them at the end of this year? Would Camden still be in the picture?

He had indeed called her as promised, full of his laid-back manner. He honestly didn't seem upset about their no-sex arrangement. She had fully expected him to bolt. Men seemed to think that sex was automatic with almost all male/female interactions. She blamed it on all the hook-up apps. They were literally there to get you a "hook-up" at any time of the day. If you were bored and wanted company, there were apps to find someone who was close by. Men had lost the art of waiting or working for it.

Although, as she had told him, this wasn't a test or some pre-determined time frame she had in mind. She was falling fast for him and that was *her* problem. She hadn't been in love...well since her last failed relationship several years ago. Frankly, this felt different and whatever it was, it scared her on a deeper level. Yet she was drawn to him, even when the safe thing would be to stay away. Luckily for her Camden didn't seem to be going anywhere...for now. They had plans to have lunch on Wednesday and she was looking forward to it. Sighing, she saw that it was almost six and decided to call Mika before it got late.

Mika answered after a few rings. "Hey, there she is! Ms. I'm gone ignore my best friend."

"Whatever. What you doing?"

"Drinking wine."

"It's only six o'clock."

"Which means it's after five, so what's your point?"

"Touché, you right."

"You know I got to prepare for the work week. Anyway, stop stalling. What happened after I left?"

"I slept with him," Andrea blurted out and had to snatch the phone from her ear, as she heard sputtering and cursing. "You okay?"

"Damn it, you made me spit red wine all over my white couch!"

"I told you not to get that couch. You are too messy to have white furniture."

"That's why they made stain guard and I paid for it. Won't help my shirt though." Mika was already in the kitchen grabbing paper towel. She decided to just take the whole roll with her. "Now, back up. I left you with the man who you almost refused to see, and you end up sleeping with him? Walk me through that progression."

Andrea walked her through the club and gave her an abridged version of the car and ended with her asking to go inside.

"You go girl! I'm so proud of you! So, was it good?"

"Mika...it was...fantastic! The best I've ever had."

Her admission left Mika silent on the other end, until she finally said, "Well, damn...no wonder you were out of commission. I'd do a slow clap, if I didn't have this glass in my hand. Matter of fact, I need another drink, because I'm getting worked up imagining sex that good."

Andrea hesitated, but who else could she talk to about this? "I uh...told him I wanted to slow down. That I didn't want to have sex again for a while."

Mika spit out another mouthful of wine. What the hell had she just heard? She reached for the paper towel again as she tried to understand what was wrong with her friend.

Andrea heard more cursing from afar, like the phone had been thrown down. "Hello? What are you doing over there?"

"Apparently, wasting all this good wine. I am *so* glad I don't have carpet. Now, what in the hell are *you* doing? You have the best sex ever, and we established before it's been a *long* time since you had any. Even longer, than your last date. And the first thing you do is tell him you don't want any more? Did he think you were crazy as hell, cause I do."

"I know it's weird. You have to understand, what he made me feel in the bedroom was unexpected. We connected in more than a sexual way. I'm basically freaking out over here! Mika...I think I'm catching feelings...like *big time* feelings and I've only been talking to him for two weeks."

"Oh. I didn't see that coming. You don't catch feelings easily. Hmm...how did he take your reversal on sex? I mean, is he still in the picture at this point?"

"Yeah he is, and that's freaking me out too. He took it very well. He forced me out for breakfast the morning after. Called me like he said he would today and we already have plans for the middle of the week."

"And he's not acting mad?" Mika asked, disbelieving.

"No, he's acting normal. A little flirtier than he was beforehand, but the same."

"Wow."

"I know."

"So, you telling me," Mika paused for effect. "That he might actually be a 'good' guy?" They had a running joke for the last few years that all the good guys were far and few in-between or married.

"Yeah...I think he might be," Andrea said quietly. This was problematic, because *real* good guys had the potential to break her heart.

It was two weeks later, on a Friday in the second week of October, when Cam walked through the restaurant to meet Robert.

"Look at that, you made it! Not brushing me off tonight I see." Robert decided to do a little fishing as Cam sat down. "Surprised you not seeing your girl today."

"Naw, we hitting a movie tomorrow night."

"Okay. Glad to see the streak of actual dates continue."

Cam just ignored him, looking over the menu.

"Are you sleeping with her yet?"

Cam jerked his eyes up from the menu to look at Robert for a moment. He halfway opened his mouth, then just shook his head and went back to reviewing the menu.

"Well?" Robert pushed, partly to annoy Cam and partly because he wanted to know.

"It's...complicated." Cam attempted to change the subject. "What are you going to order?"

Robert tossed his menu aside, letting Cam know that he wasn't about to be put off the subject. "What does that mean, *complicated?* Usually the answer is a simple "yes" or "no". Yes, I hit that or naw, I haven't hit it yet. Which one is it?"

It was Cam's turn to toss his menu down and glower across the table. He didn't like Robert's tone. "It's the 'none of your damn business' one. Drop it."

The two friends started at each other, Cam on the verge of being upset and Robert bemused, yet stubborn. Finally, Robert shrugged his shoulders like he didn't have a care in the world. "O-kay...whatever works. I'm gone try this Marco Polo burger and get a drink. What you drinking? I got you."

The tension in Cam's shoulders relaxed and he sat back in his chair, picking up the menu. In the language of men, offering to buy a drink was the equivalent of an apology. He accepted, as he wasn't quite sure why Robert's teasing had bothered him so much in the first place.

Robert moved the conversation away from Andrea, yet in his mind he was mildly concerned. He got the message loud and clear that things were serious with her and Cam. He just didn't think Cam understood *how* serious. Cam had never gotten this upset due to regular ribbing over a woman. Nor had he ever been shy about sharing basic sexual information. While they were old enough not to go into detail about their sexual exploits, they'd never held back the simple answer of whether or not they were sleeping with someone. Add that to his ambiguous answer of "it's complicated", and Robert just hoped his friend knew what he was doing.

Chapter Ten

Cam slung the towel around his neck, walking up from the basement after his workout. He was working out more than usual for two reasons. One, it was almost the end of October and he was trying to get an early start on keeping in shape during the winter months to come. After all, he could actually do something about winter fat. His second reason was a whole lot harder to manage.

Andrea weighed on his mind during the day and especially the nights. Working out was a way to expel the pent up sexual energy he had. In the month since their night together they regularly saw each other several times a week. Wednesday had become their standard day for a lunch outing. While Friday or Saturday, and sometimes both, were their date night, most weeknights they talked on the phone as well. On days they didn't speak, a text message conversation usually took place.

Since he saw or spoke to her all the time now, that wasn't the problem. The problem was his body hadn't gotten the memo that there was no sex to be had. Mentally, he didn't have a problem with her decision. While he didn't understand completely why she wanted to end the scorching sex they could be having, he respected her choice. Physically, he just couldn't seem to get the message. To be fair, he was just a man after all, who had tasted what was now forbidden, and damn if he didn't want to taste it again.

He'd kept his promise not to push but he sure as hell did his best to ramp up the mood enough so that she'd want him back in her bed. He touched her as much as possible, regardless of where they were. He held her hand, stroked her waist, and kissed her cheek whenever he could get away with it. In private, they often spent time before or after a date chilling at each other's houses. This usually resulted in a make-out session that could be as tame as kisses or exciting as bare skin with hot hands and tongues. Really, was there any wonder his libido was confused?

Just as he'd told Robert a couple of weeks ago, it was complicated. He was in a rough spot sexually and mentally. He'd thought a lot about the "almost" argument he'd had with his friend, and finally figured out why the regular guy talk had bothered him. Simple answer...it was Andrea. She was different. He'd known almost from the start but hadn't wanted to admit it. If he had only cared about getting in her pants, most likely he would be gone by now.

However with her, he wanted more than just sex. He wanted her to come to him, certain in both mind and body. He couldn't...*wouldn't* put a name to it...not quite yet. He'd sent flowers to her job the Monday after they'd slept together, not to get in her good graces but because he felt she deserved them. The one thing he knew clearly, was that he wanted her in his life. His days were better and lighter when he teased her serious personality into a laugh or a smile.

He also enjoyed the conversations they had, whether they were about politics, current events, or debating taste in music. Simply put, he liked her. He didn't begrudge any time he could spend with her, sex or no sex. He justified not telling his best friend any of this because he didn't think he'd understand. Robert was more rigid in how he handled relationships with women. It was usually on his terms or nothing at all. He wouldn't understand why Cam was *more* than willing to be flexible and do whatever it took to win Andrea for good.

Halloween fell on a Tuesday this year and Andrea had almost completely forgotten about it. She wasn't really into costumes, whether they be on kids or adults, but she didn't hate the holiday either. The best part of it for her, was watching scary movies. She had tried handing out candy the first year she'd had her house. She'd never do that again! In her neighborhood, the procession of kids seemed to never stop. She had run out of her generous supply of candy within two hours! Today, she was just happy to be walking into her house at a quarter to six. She made sure her porch light was off, before shucking her shoes and heading to the bedroom to undress.

She had talked to Camden while driving home, after he'd made sure that she was using her hands-free speaker.

"What you got planned for tonight?" He'd asked.

"Absolutely nothing. Might watch some of my fav horror movies but that's it. What about you. You doing trick or treating?"

He'd laughed before answering. "Yeah, I plan to do a little treating tonight."

"But no tricks huh?"

"Well now, that all depends on who's asking?"

"You a mess!"

"Yeah, but you like it. Look, let me let you go. I got a couple of more errands to run. You have a good night."

"Okay. You too."

She'd arrived home not long after they hung up. Now an half an hour later and fresh out the shower, she poured herself a glass of wine and went to pick out a few movies. She would figure out what to eat after. She'd just pulled out the 2004 *Dawn of the Dead*, *28 Days Later* and *28 Weeks Later* movies, when she heard her doorbell ring.

"Who in the heck? I swear, it better not be some teenager. They know what the light being out means." Placing the movies on the table, she walked irritably to the door. The thought to ignore it ran through her head, but the bell rang again and she was annoyed enough that she wanted to give whoever it was a piece of her mind.

"Don't you see my light is off?" She was already saying as she jerked open the front door.

"I noticed. I actually almost tripped up your steps because of it."

"Camden!"

"I brought you a treat." He held up a large pizza box in one hand, a six pack of brew and a plastic bag in the other. When she just looked at him with her mouth open, he added, "Can I come in?"

"You...I wasn't expecting you."

"Come on...it ruins the treat if I can't even get in the door."

"Yeah, come in. I really thought you were some kid being a smart ass." She backed up and let him in before following him into the living room. "What are you doing here?"

"Thought I'd surprise you with dinner. I was hoping I could watch some movies with you." He saw the uncertain look on her face. "Or not." He placed the pizza and beer on the table. "I can drop off the goodies and leave...though I'm taking the beer with me."

"No, no. You can stay, it just caught me off guard. I'm not even dressed." She fluttered her hand to her head, her hair already wrapped in a black scarf.

After all, she hadn't been planning on going anywhere for the rest of the night, nor had she been expecting visitors. She'd put on some shape-hugging joggers for warmth and a purple, long-sleeved breast cancer awareness shirt, from a walk she'd participated in earlier in the month.

Ahh, Cam thought to himself. She was reluctant about him seeing her in her chill mode clothes. To date, he'd only seen her in after work or date ensembles. Even the few times they'd did Netflix and chill, she hadn't been dressed this causally. With just the plastic bag in his hand, he walked over to her and gave her a kiss.

"You look fine to me, but then again, you always do. You at home, you're dressed exactly how you should be. What do you say? Let's have a relaxing Halloween."

Andrea looked into his mirth-filled eyes and let her apprehension go. He was right. Since he showed up unannounced, he got what he got. Besides, as usual, she seemed to be the only one who cared about something so trivial.

"Fine, but only because you brought me pizza."

"I got half-and-half." He knew she was a cheese, green peppers, and chicken type of girl, while he preferred a manly meat lover's.

"Good!" She gave him her first smile of the night. "What's in the bag?"

"Don't worry about it. You go put on a movie. I'll bring us some plates." He gave her a push towards the couch, by way of her backside. Copping a feel and getting her moving, while he went in the kitchen. He tossed his coat over a kitchen chair and a couple minutes later, he walked back in, carrying some paper plates, napkins, and the bottle of wine she'd opened, along with a medium plastic bowl.

"Let me help before you drop something." Andrea jumped up and grabbed her wine and the bowl, placing both on the table. She looked down and saw it filled with assorted candy. "Camden, we can't eat all this candy! You'll have me sick."

He got settled in and pulled her close. "That's the whole point of Halloween right? Get sick eating candy. We'll pig out and watch folks make stupid choices in these horror films."

Andrea couldn't help but laugh at that. "Sounds like a prefect Halloween to me."

It was the best Halloween she'd had since she was a kid. They'd demolished the pizza before the *Dawn of the Dead* characters even made it to the mall. During *28 Days Later*, they'd started in on the candy while she alternated between laughing and jumping at the images onscreen. She liked watching horror movies with him! He spent the movie pointing out the things the characters did wrong or how they deserved to die. Nothing seemed to bother him. Though he had seemed freaked out by how fast the Zombies had been at the end of the first movie, shouting out *"Oh hell no! That shit ain't fair, they running around like Usain Bolt!"*

By the time they put in the last movie, they were both stretched out on her couch snuggled together. She loved the solid feel of him. Being able to totally relax with him was something she treasured. She was able to let her hair down, or in this case, keep it wrapped up around him.

He joked around with her a lot, and when she returned the favor, he never took offense. She tended to be on the serious side, which was why she and Mika made such good friends. They balanced each other out. Camden brought out her lighter side as well, and overall she just felt good around him. As the last movie of the night was nearing the end, she was more concerned with how good he felt, than if the bad ass kids were going to make it to the helicopter or not.

He probably wouldn't believe her, but she found it *very* hard not to give in to her urges. She thought about their night together several times a week. No matter how hard she tried, she couldn't forget how his lips had felt kissing up her thighs, his tongue licking up her middle. Invariably, those thoughts reminded her of the way he felt inside her. Just the thought of his powerful strokes had her squirming next to him.

She slid her hands low until she was toying with the top of his pants. He didn't have on a belt and she teased her finger underneath his waistband. She felt him tense, then relax. They'd fooled around plenty. He'd gone down on her several more times, to her dismay and delight. She'd played with him as well, but he'd never let her bring him to completion with a hand job. Giving head had never been her favorite thing to do, but she'd given it willingly to her long term boyfriends for special occasions. Andrea had contemplated going down on Cam a couple of times, and thought maybe she'd try it tonight to pay him back for the delightful evening.

When Cam felt her hand slide fully down his pants and grab his penis, he sucked in a breath. "You looking for something down my pants?"

"Yeah...and I think I found it." She gave him a squeeze and he grunted before kissing the life out of her.

That's all they needed for an intense round of groping and kissing to ensue. After a while, she pushed up the thin sweater he was wearing and flicked her fingers over his nipples, making him shudder.

"Thought I was the only one *treating* tonight," he asked her.

"I don't know...there might be some type of *tricking*, too." She gave him a naughty smile, kissing his chin before sliding down his body to run her tongue over his now sensitive chest. She kissed her way down his stomach, then got the button of his pants undone and the zipper pulled down before he suddenly sat up.

Cam knew this was "Devil's Night", but he wasn't going to place himself in hell by letting her give him a blowjob. There was no way he'd be able to back off after that. It was better not to take the chance of ruining the night. He hauled her up for a deep kiss, trying to distract her before he said, "The movie is over."

"Oh." She hadn't noticed, but glancing at the TV saw the credits rolling.

"It's almost one in the morning. I should be going." Cam moved her aside. "You have work tomorrow." He stood up fixing his pants, before collecting their trash and heading to the kitchen.

Andrea watched him go with a confused frown on her face. She knew he hadn't mistaken where her mouth was headed. Strangely, she felt disappointed about not being able to go down on him. She stood up and met him coming out of the kitchen with his coat already on. Opening her mouth to protest, he cut her off with a quick kiss before walking quickly to the door.

"I'll text you when I get home. Have a good day tomorrow."

"Yeah, you too," she mumbled, following him to the door and locking up. As she heard his car start, she shook her head in annoyance. "Great, Zombies don't scare him, but the thought of me giving him head runs him off."

Chapter Eleven

Almost a month had passed since her failed attempt to give Camden fellatio, and she was starting to think Camden was losing interest, at least in having sex with *her*. While she may not have as much relationship experience as most women her age, she wasn't stupid. If he was no longer interested in getting it from her, then that meant he was probably getting it from someone else.

Since that night, he backed away from getting as physical with her. Oh, they still kissed, and there was light touching, but that was it. Clothes stayed on, and nobody's mouth was on anyone's naughty parts. They still talked and saw each other the same amount, everything was the same expect the physical part. That was starting to be a problem for her.

She gave a deep sigh before noticing she was chewing her pen top again. In frustration, she tossed it across her office until it hit the door with an audible ping. When her phone rang an instant later, it made her jump. She snatched up the phone without even looking.

"Hello," she said shortly.

"Whoa, bad day?"

"Sorry Cam, I didn't know it was you." She was so caught off guard, that she forgot to tease him by using his full name.

"They messing with you over at PWC? Who is it? I'll come over there if I have to."

And just like that he was surprising a laugh out of her. That was why she loved talking to him. "Oh, really? You can come over here and get me fired?"

"Hey, I'll catch them out in the parking lot. They'll never know what hit them...literally."

"Well luckily for them you won't be needed. No one did anything to me. It's just been a long day."

"Well it's almost over. Are you able to leave on time tonight?"

Andrea looked at her computer screen and saw that it was three o'clock. "Yeah, I should be able to leave on time, though I'll be bringing home work this weekend."

"We'll sit around working together, as I need to finish up this small project."

"Sounds like a work date to me. You want me to come to your place after work tonight?" Andrea asked.

"That works. Look, I won't take up much more of your time. I wanted to ask you something about next week."

"Shoot."

"Will you be in town for Thanksgiving?"

"Umm, actually I will. I trade off turkey day and Christmas with visiting my family. This year, they don't get a visit until December."

"Sucks for them, but lucky for me."

"And why is that, Mr. Holden?"

"So you can go with me to a Thanksgiving dinner. It's a tradition for me to stop in at Robert's place, for a few hours."

She didn't need to ask why he wouldn't be visiting his own family. She knew he wasn't particularly close to the family he still had in the area. She'd also come to know that his best friend was more like a brother, so it didn't surprise her that he would spend a holiday with him. What she *was* surprised by, was that he was asking her to come. But what did it mean that he wanted her to meet what was essentially his family?

As if he could read her thoughts through the silence on the line, he said, "It's honestly not a big deal. It's a causal gathering. Usually never more than twelve to fifteen people. He has a small, immediate family that gets together. I'd really like you to come with me, if you have a few hours free that day."

Why was she even hesitating? Hadn't she just been thinking he was losing interest? This invitation had to be a good thing. Not to mention she was curious about meeting his friend. She wanted to know what type of man Camden considered a best friend.

"You know, I'd love to go. I'm not doing anything that day and I had no other plans. Thanks for asking."

"Good. I'm glad you'll be able to go. His family is great. We'll talk details next week."

"Cool. See you later around 5:30ish?"

"Yeah. I'll pick up something to eat. Just text me what you want."

"Okay." As he started to say goodbye, she rushed to keep him on the line. "Hey, Camden?"

"Yeah?"

"Thanks for wanting to be my defender earlier."

"You called me Cam when you answered the phone...you know that will make me do anything for you."

"Bye Camden." She hung up the phone with his chuckle still ringing in her ear.

Andrea had been so busy that it seemed like she blinked, and Thanksgiving was upon them. They would be arriving a little after four, as Camden claimed dinner usually started after the football game.

"*Most times, I try not to arrive until the Detroit Lions game is over. Robert is a sports fan. He and his cousins take it a bit too seriously for me. This way we can arrive when the theatrics are over.*"

During that conversation, he had also assured her she didn't need to make anything. When she insisted, he'd told her to bring some Hennessey for the guys and some wine for the ladies. She had taken his advice, making her shopping list easy. Now, they were on their way to Robert's house in Royal Oak.

When they arrived she wasn't surprised by the big modern house, it was the norm for this particular city. There were a number of cars already in the semi-circle driveway, so Camden parked on the street. When they got out, he reached into the back seat and pulled out something wrapped in aluminum foil.

"What is that?" she asked suspiciously.

"My Baileys pound cake. I make it every year."

"You told me not to bring anything!"

"You're a guest, guest don't bring anything." Cam laughed as a cute little pout graced her lips. "Stop pouting before they think you stuck up or something."

"You know what!" She snapped her mouth shut and put on a smile as the door opened to reveal a tall, dark-skinned brother.

"About time you got here. I don't know why you don't come for the game."

"For what? To see the same old slaughtering of the Lions and hear your mouth? I'll pass." They joked, while giving each other the one-armed hugs men were known for, all the while being careful of the cake in Cams hand.

The man hugging Camden then turned to her, cocking his head to the side and giving her a small, skeptical smile. "You must be Andrea of the 'pretty eyes'." He stuck out his hand. "Nice to meet you."

80

"Thanks for allowing me to celebrate with your family. It's nice to meet you as well. I've heard a lot about you."

"Same here."

Robert turned back to Cam and snatched the cake out his hand. "Give me that cake before you drop it. Come on in out of the cold. We should be eating soon."

As they followed him through the house, Andrea didn't pay attention to her surroundings. She felt Camden's best friend's greeting had been a little cool...or was it her imagination? It was always a little unnerving meeting important people in someone else's life. The noise of a TV and children laughing did reach her however, as well as the aroma of the meal. Those things reminded her this was a holiday gathering, and she should relax and try to enjoy it.

They reached the large, modern kitchen that had an open layout so you could see into the living room. She saw a number of kids of all ages and a couple of men sitting around the couch. Camden took the bag of liquor out her hand and handed it to Robert, as Robert handed the cake to a black woman of average height, who leaned past him to kiss Camden on the cheek. The woman turned her eyes to Andrea and gave her a warm smile. She was about to say something, when she was cut off.

"Baby, what you got in that other bag?"

Andrea turned towards one of the other two women in the kitchen. "Some wine ma'am, I hope that's okay."

"Of course it's okay, we drink in this family." The woman all but snatched the bag out her hand. "Moderately, of course. I can't stand a drunk. I'm Dolores by the way. Roberts's mother's older sister."

"You're my *only* sister. I don't know why you always got to add the 'older' part." She grabbed Andrea's hand and gave it a squeeze while rolling her eyes in her sister's direction. "I'm Johanna. Very nice to meet a friend of Cam's."

"Nice to meet you as well. I'm Andrea. Camden told me not to bring anything, but I feel bad. I'm decent in the kitchen, do you need help with anything?"

"Oh, you can cook?" Dolores raised an eyebrow at the statement.

"Yes ma'am I can cook pretty well.

"Ha! Brihanna you hear that!" Dolores shouted over her shoulder to the younger woman in the kitchen, who was stirring a pot at the stove. "This is a woman not much older than you probably, who can at least do a little something in the kitchen. What's your excuse?"

"I don't need to cook when I know how to call a carry-out number."

"I've told you to leave my girl alone." Johanna said, before turning and waving her hand at the two men watching the conversation with amusement. "You two get out this kitchen. Make sure the table is set, we should be ready to eat in about ten minutes or so."

Chapter Twelve

After the two men left, Andrea was left facing three women who all looked at her curiously. She knew she was in for a grilling, the kind that women did so well. She figured it was fair, since Camden had put up with Mika's twenty-one questions. At least Johanna was looking at her in a warm and friendly manner. Dolores was looking at her shrewdly, and Brihanna gave her a look of pity and shook her head.

"So, how long have you known Cam?"

"Technically, since the end of August, Ms. Johanna."

"Honey, we are not formal, though I thank you for having manners. You can just call us by our first names. Cam is such a good boy. We're always pleased to have him."

"I don't know why you keep calling those men *boys*. They both thirty," Dolores muttered.

"Well Robert is my baby boy, and Cam might as well be my son. So I can call them what I want to call them."

"Humph." Dolores ignored her sister and addressed Andrea. "You two serious?"

"I, uhh..." How to answer that? She and Camden talked about many things, except defining their relationship, which she didn't mind for now. "We're dating. Spending a lot of time together." They all just looked at her until she gave a shy smile and shook her head. "We're friends."

Johanna's smile widened. "Well, that's a wonderful place to start!"

"Could have fooled me. You two look closer than just friends."

"Aunt Dolores!"

"What?" She threw up her hands in Brihanna's direction. "You young people have such dirty minds. I meant the way he was acting with her. He wasn't acting that way with anyone else he's brought."

"Oh...and how many has he brought exactly?" The bite in Andrea's voice had the three women's heads whipping toward her.

"What my Aunt was trying to say, before she put her foot in it, was that he seems to be closer to you than the other two women we've met."

"How so?"

"The way he looks at you for one," Johanna said softly.

"I saw how he had his hand on your back the entire time too. Standing extra close to you," Dolores piped in.

When Andrea looked at Brihanna, the younger woman just shrugged. "I'll reserve my final judgement for now."

"Well, I'm not sure what you ladies saw that quickly, but we're taking it slow."

The two sisters gave each other a look before Johanna said, "That's never a bad thing...I guess. Anyway, we're glad to have you. Now, let's go feed these men and kids before they riot."

The rest of the evening went by fast. She met Robert's four cousins. Devon and Darrell, Edward, his wife and kids and Thomas and his two kids. Dinner was delicious and lively, and Andrea had no problem relaxing. She was seeing a different side of Camden as he joked easily with all of the men as they talked sports, work, and other topics. They sat next to each other, and whenever he wasn't eating he had his hand on her back, shoulder, or neck. Once or twice, she saw the sisters looking at each other and smirking.

Robert, who was sitting across from them, also gave her a few speculative looks. She tried to ignore the scrutiny as the day continued. It was great to see how Camden moved within this family setting. He seemed to be well known and well-liked by everyone. The kids and young adults seemed to gravitate towards him and value his opinion. At the same time, he didn't seem bothered that they wanted some of his attention. He gladly gave it, though this didn't really surprise her, as she knew how patient he could be.

After dinner and some conversation, the men took the kids into the living room and a video game tournament ensued. That's when the women headed back to the kitchen and sat around the center island, drinking a variety of wines and having a second helping of dessert. An hour after that, all six men walked through the kitchen dressed for the outdoors. Camden walked up to her, giving her a quick kiss on the forehead, as if it was something he did all the time, which it was...but only in private.

"We going outside for a bit." He threw a look over his shoulder at her. "I won't be long. Then we can head out."

"Take your time. I'm in no rush." She gave him a smile and a shrug.

The men collected her liquor contribution from the counter, along with some insulated mugs, and headed through the house to Robert's back deck. Once their footsteps receded, she felt all eyes on her.

She found herself laughing and shaking her head. "No one say nothing!"

"As much as I hate to say this...and trust me, I do." Brihanna took a big gulp of wine. "Mom and Aunt Dolores were totally right."

The men spread out around the back patio. While there was no snow on the ground this year, it was still cold with temperatures in the mid-thirties. This was normal, as the temperature dropped quickly in the evening, and it was already closing in on six thirty. The back lights were set to turn on come dusk, so they had plenty of light.

Devon, better known as "Dev" was looking at the bottle of liquor. "Man, your lady got taste *and* money. She got us the LVHM brand."

"Stop caressing the thing and open it, before my balls freeze off," Darrell grumbled.

"You got circulation problems? What you not getting no action lately? Gotta keep the blood flowing!" Edward baited his youngest brother as Dev passed around the bottle.

"Hell nawl! The chick I was talking to for the last couple of months wanted to talk about her relationship goals." Darrell shook his head disgustedly. "She was expecting a ring at the six-month mark. As you can guess, we were *not* on the same page, so that was that. I've been getting zero action for the last month."

"Man, it's rough…two months for me," Cam mumbled, unfortunately not low enough.

"What was that I heard?" Robert loudly asked, getting everyone's attention. "Cam, did you say it's been two months for you? You finally ready to share with the class or not?" Robert was looking forward to finally getting some real information on what exactly was going on with those two.

Cam gave him a dirty look and downed his shot of Henny to stall for time, but apparently, they had no plans to give him any, as he heard Thomas say, "Wait a minute. You bringing that fine woman to holiday dinners but not getting none? What madness is this?"

Cam scowled at him too, then snatched the bottle from the person to his left and poured more into his cup. "She…we're taking it slow." There was no way he was telling them that they'd slept together, before she'd called a halt. There would be a litany of unflattering jokes at his expense. He wasn't sure they would ever let him live it down.

They all looked at him before busting out laughing, though Robert just stared at him.

"You had it right the first time, brother. *She* taking it slow. You know you want a piece of that." Dev threw the comment at him and the laughter increased.

"Of course I do, but if she wants to wait, we'll wait. She's worth it."

That cut the laughter off abruptly, as all the men looked at each other. Thomas glanced at Robert before clearing his throat. "Do you know what you getting yourself into?"

"It's not that big of a deal. I've gone longer, when I've been in-between girlfriends."

"Key word there is 'in-between'. You got a woman now. You can't tell me that's not hard?" Dev questioned.

"Yeah, especially when you spend all your time with her." Robert said, taking a slow sip of the fine cognac. If Cam kept knocking back a brand this expensive so fast, he wouldn't be able to drive. His overdrinking was a sign to Robert that this subject bothered him more than he was willing to admit.

"It can be hard sometimes, but it's not killing me. I'll survive."

"Hell, lack of sex is already affecting your cognitive ability!" Darrell shot out. "There is no way I could constantly be around that woman and *know* that I'm not getting those legs wrapped around me. Shit would drive me crazy!"

Edward, smacked Darrel in the arm. "Hey, watch your mouth." Darrell had never been in a serious relationship yet. He didn't realize how close he was to an ass-whoopin, if the tightening of Cam's mouth and fist was any indication.

"What *we* do is working for us," Cam said tightly.

"And that's all that matters," Edward soothed. "As the only one with a wife −"

Thomas cut in. "You're not the only one who had a wife."

"My bad. As the only one who got a wife and *kept* her...it only matters what works for you two. Every relationship is different. She seems like a fine lady."

"Yeah, real fine," Darrell mumbled, then louder to Cam, "Man, look if you need pointers, there's no shame coming to me. I'd be happy to help you out."

Cam took a sip of drink instead of a gulp this time, then smiled. "If I wanted advice, I'd go to Dev's ass way before you."

Dev reached over and gave him some dap.

"Devon? Man, are you crazy? I taught him everything he knows. Sadly, he sucked as a pupil!" Robert made the dig, and just like that the tension was broken.

The men went on to laugh and talk for another half an hour, almost finishing the big bottle of Hennessey, until they heard a knock on the patio glass door.

Andrea opened the door and peeked out. When she noticed how little was left in the bottle, she shook her head, then smiled around at the group of men. "I see my gift was appreciated at least. Camden, Johanna wanted me to see what you wanted on your to-go plate?"

Cam stood up quickly and the alcohol hit him. "Let me go in before she piles everything on my plate. Robert, your mom acts like I'm a starving kitten."

"That means she likes you."

"Also..." Andrea aimed her comment at the other men as she watched Camden stumble towards her. "Dolores said, and I'm quoting, 'Tell the rest of them to get in this house before they catch their death'."

The rest of the men stood up with a little grumbling, but it was clear none of them had any intention of defying the order.

Robert caught up to Cam and Andrea then said to her, "I think you'll need to drive home to be on the safe side."

Cam looked at Robert. "I'll be all right."

Robert continued to look at Andrea. "Don't forget what city you in. You should drive."

"Not a problem. I don't mind. I stopped drinking when ya'll went outside with that bottle."

"Good. You got to take care of our boy."

Chapter Thirteen

The Saturday night after Thanksgiving found Andrea laying on her couch reading a book when her cell phone rang. She saw who it was and enthusiastically picked up. She needed to talk.

"Hey! I'm glad you called and made it back safe. How's your family?" Mika's family did a mini-retreat for Thanksgiving each year.

"It was good! Nobody got on my nerves this time, and the drive was good too. My cousins are my cousins. The parents are all doing well of course. Enough about me, though. I called you so I could detox from my family visit, not relive it. Did you go to the spa or just relax?"

"I did get a massage on Friday. I actually spent Thanksgiving with Camden."

"Say what now?"

"Before you start, I honestly...mostly...forgot about it. You know how work is crazy right before a holiday."

Mika cut her off. "Yeah, yeah. Skip the excuses and tell me how this came about. I can't believe you didn't tell me you were meeting his family."

"That's because I really didn't."

Mika rubbed her temples and tried to keep her annoyance to a minimum. "Andrea, you know I love you right...but I will punch you like I did my one cousin two Thanksgivings ago, if you don't start speaking in complete sentences."

"You would *try*." When her friend just remained silent on the phone, Andrea sighed. "Sorry okay. He's not close to the family he has here, but he asked me to go over his best friend's house for the holiday."

"*Now* we getting somewhere. So, you finally met the best friend! How did that go?"

"Robert? It went okay. He was a little chilly, in my opinion. He didn't grill me like you did Camden at least. He left that for his mom, aunt, and sister to do."

"Oh, ignore the friend. Men act real sensitive when they think they're losing a friend to a woman. More importantly, you got the concerned 'women of the family' treatment. Things must be getting serious."

"Why does everyone keep saying that?"

"Who besides me is saying it?"

"All the women in Robert's family. They seem to think Camden was treating me differently, more seriously than anyone else they'd met."

"Hmm, well they know him better than you, unless they were just trying to be nice."

"They are a very outspoken and genuine family. I liked them a lot actually. I think they were just telling the truth as they saw it. They just got it wrong is all."

"What did Cam have to say about it?"

"Nothing! I didn't mention what they said to him."

"Why not? Never mind...so did you spend the rest of the holiday break with him too?"

"No, he was called in at the last moment on an important project out of town. I've talked to him since Thursday, but he's been preparing and trying to get up to speed with the little information they sent him. He leaves tomorrow. He said the company is putting him up at the downtown Hilton in Los Angeles. I told him at least they got him really good digs."

"How long is he going to be gone for?"

"He said a full week."

Mika heard the displeasure in her friend's voice over the phone and smiled ruefully. "That man is so gone on you. If Thanksgiving wasn't a clue, this sure is. He wants to make sure his boo-baby knows where he's at!"

"None of that means much."

"If you don't stop saying ridiculous things to me. I *know* you are not that clueless, cause I wouldn't be friends with someone who is. Don't no man who don't like you give you his hotel info while he's on a business trip if he doesn't care for you."

"I guess you right, he did make a point to tell me all of it in advance."

"Of course I'm right. Are you finally giving him some again?"

"No, not yet."

"What exactly are you waiting on? He treats you right and seems to want a serious relationship with you."

"I know, I know. He really is great. We get close sometimes, but it never seems to happen." Andrea thought again about how sexually distant he'd been lately.

"Andrea, *you* betta make it happen. You trust me to give you the truth right? So, I'm going to give it to you. You got a good man who happens to be fine as well. Who is A-Okay that you slowed things down. He's what most black women would outright cut you over. He's also the type, successful white women would feel okay taking home to daddy. Now, it's clear that he likes you for you. Isn't in it, to hit it and quit it, but even the most patient man has limits. You know women seem to be able to smell when a man has a woman. You're making it *easier* for fine upstanding Cam to be *tempted*, is all I'm saying."

Andrea actually sucked her teeth at Mika's tirade. "You finished?"

"Yeah...no I'm not. Let me put it plainly, stop teasing that man!"

"I'm not being a tease! I resent that. I've been honest and upfront with him. He can walk away if he doesn't like it."

"Okay." Mika softened her voice. "I take it back. You're not teasing him. But you *are* torturing yourself. You need to trust him...no better yet, trust *yourself* to be with him."

It was Andrea's turn to get quiet on the phone. Finally, she said, "I'm trying...I really am."

Cam had left for L.A. the Sunday after Thanksgiving. He was semi pissed that the one week trip had turned into two. He'd called Andrea to let her know his time would be extended, and her voice had sounded just as disappointed as he felt. Cam was missing Andrea, and was man enough to admit it. He'd gotten accustomed to seeing her on a regular basis. He was busy getting as much information as he could for this rush project, so that excessive stays like this wouldn't be needed again.

Because he was so busy, they barely spoke. Their conversations were limited to a few minutes at a time, and they tried to fill in the gaps with a few emails and texts. He was finding it wasn't the same as seeing her or touching her. Halfway through the second week, he was itching to get back, and that was a departure from the norm. In the past he hadn't minded some travel here and there. After all, it was on the company's dime and he usually found time to chill and explore a little before he left. Once in a while, when exploring he had found an interesting woman to help the hours go by. Some he'd even kept in touch with for a while.

Now, there was only one woman he wanted to get back to, just to see her face. He had to wonder if she thought about him, half as much as he did her. Oh, he knew she was feeling him, as they always had a great time together. It was easy between them. They were in sync most of the time. She wasn't "easy" like those women who never had their own opinion, who never argued, and were so thirsty for a man they agreed to pretty much everything.

No, she was easy in the sense that she didn't argue just to argue, but she made her thoughts and ideas known. She could be shy or serious at times, yet always had a genuine laugh at his teasing and jokes, even when they happened to be corny. She had a quiet confidence to her that showed in how she carried herself, yet she could be silly and have fun when she was given the chance to. Cam sighed and got back to work. If he wasn't careful, he'd spend all day thinking about her.

Andrea had thought a lot about Mika's words in the almost two weeks that Camden had been gone. Now, as she lay in bed on Wednesday night, she realized the time he'd been away had made a few things clear to her. First, she was way too comfortable with him being a part of her life. She was missing him like crazy! She was just realizing how often they touched base in some form. More importantly, she was wondering why *she* was holding their relationship back from moving forward.

They had been talking technically a week after their first meeting, so since the first week of September...almost four months. Even though they hadn't had the "exclusivity" talk yet, as far as she could tell, they were a couple that spent every spare moment together. Camden was doing everything right, and had been from the very start. Damn, but Mika was right! He was a catch *inside* and *outside* the bedroom. Hell, for what he could do between the sheets alone...women would run her over, for pipe laid like that.

While she'd enjoyed sex without being one of those women who were obsessed with it, she now understood why some *might* be. Why was she denying herself mind blowing sex? She didn't know how long this thing with Camden would last, so why wasn't she enjoying the physical parts like she enjoyed everything else he offered her? More importantly, why was she denying him? If ever there was a man deserving of the cookie, it was him.

Right then, she made up her mind that the next time they were alone, she would take their fooling around right to the bedroom. She was excited that she'd made her decision, and wished she could see him now! To bad he was on the other side of the country. An idea took hold, and she sat up in bed pondering it more. Did she have the nerve? She couldn't sleep anyway. Looking at the clock, it was about nine-thirty his time, so she figured it was now or never. She spent a few minutes getting into her *costume*, so to speak, before picking up her cell phone and hitting his number. He picked up on the fourth ring.

"Hey! This is a pleasant surprise."

"Is this a bad time? Am I calling too late?"

"Never a bad time for you baby. You good. I finished up work for the night a little while ago and just got out the shower, so perfect timing. Though now that I think of it, this is late for you to be up on a Wednesday night. Is everything okay?"

"Everything is fine...well not really. I couldn't sleep. I missed you today at lunch."

"Aww baby, I missed you too. I'll be home this Friday afternoon. I can't wait to see you."

"Me either." After a pause, she asked, "What you wearing?"

"Excuse me?"

"You heard me, you said you just got out the shower. What do you got on?"

Cam literally took the phone from his ear and looked at it. Was he losing his Andrea-starved mind? "Clue me in. What's going on?"

"Nothing, since you won't tell me what you wearing. I'm trying to have phone sex with you, but you making this difficult."

Chapter Fourteen

Cam's brain froze for a minute as he tried to digest her words. Luckily, his dick didn't seem to have that problem, as it twitched to attention. Once he got his mouth closed, and could form words, he said, "Baby, say no more! Let's FaceTime so we can do this right."

Andrea grinned on the other end of the phone. "No let's do this the old-fashioned way. No video." He didn't understand how much courage this was taking her. She didn't think she could do this with his eyes on her.

"Okay, no problem. Whatever you want."

Moving forward with her half thought out plan, she lowered her voice to what she hoped was a sexy purr and demanded, "So what you got on?"

"A t-shirt and boxers, what about you?"

"A red lace bra that barely covers my aching breasts and a red lace thong to match."

"Damn...." Cam couldn't articulate anything else, as the blood flow from his brain headed south. The image of her curls playing peek a-boo through red lace and the thong string nestled firmly between her plump ass cheeks had his hand massaging his dick over his boxers.

"Take everything off." She commanded.

"You want me naked?"

"Yes, I want that firm, lean body naked. I'm hoping there are some damp spots left from the shower, so I can lick them dry."

"Damn Andrea!"

"I don't hear clothes being taken off."

"Sorry baby, I'm getting rid of them now. I promise you won't have to ask me twice again." Cam dropped the phone on the bed to whip off his t-shirt and almost tore off his boxers before picking up the phone again.

"Everything off?" Andrea questioned.

"Yes, ma'am."

"Good. Now imagine me sliding my hands all over your chest."

"Girl...hell." Cam was *slowly* stroking his shaft. "Are you touching yourself?"

"Yes, I pulled the bra down and I'm stroking my nipples."

Cam heard his shallow breathing in his own ear and didn't care. "Both?"

Andrea heard it too, and it thrilled a part of her that she was turning him on so easily. She gave a throaty chuckle before answering. "Yes, both. I'm practicing safe phone sex, since someone is a stickler for phone safety. I'm hands-free over here. Free to roam...all over."

He almost bit his tongue. Luckily, she continued. "You got some lotion near you?"

"Uhh no, but I can get some." Cam was already up rushing to bring the bottle of Jergens he'd picked up in town from the bathroom to the bed.

"Don't you need it to...you know?"

"It's not mandatory, but it does make it better."

"Then use it. I want this to be good for you," Andrea whispered in the phone, her hand sliding down her stomach. "I want to make you cum."

"Damn! You almost just did!" Cam tightened his hold around his shaft before taking her advice and adding some lotion. He started to stroke in earnest. "Where your hands at now?"

"One is pinching my nipple and the other is headed down south."

"Mmm...you still got those panties on?"

"Yes," she said breathily, as her hand slid over the lace, rubbing it against her hot button. The scratchy contrast had her shivering.

"Take 'em off...no better yet, slide them down just to your knees. Then spread your thighs as much as you can."

Andrea hurried to comply as her heart jumped in her chest. "Okay."

"Slide two fingers from the top down and part those pretty lips for me, until your clit is firmly pinched by them. Tell me how it feels."

Andrea arched her back against the pillows as she touched herself. "It feels good, baby."

"I bet. Take those fingers lower and dip 'em in that wetness I know is there." Cam's voice was deep and gravelly as his hand tightened on his cock.

"Ooh...Cam!"

He wasn't sure if it was her groan or the use of his name that did it for him, but suddenly he didn't know if he could last much longer. "Ah baby girl, you got a vibrator right?"

"I...what?" Now Andrea was the one having problems thinking, as her fingers turned her on. "I have one, but..."

"I'm not gone last much longer, but I want you to cum before I do. Do as I say and get your vibrator out."

Sitting up from the bed at the growled command, she didn't know when he'd taken over this encounter, but she was okay with it. "Okay! I'm getting it." She was shaking with need, and luckily only had to roll to the bedside table to retrieve one of her toys. "Okay, I got it."

"Good...good, turn it on, let me hear it." Cam had taken the time waiting to add more lotion to his rock-hard penis. He had a feeling he was going to need it. When he heard the rumbling of her toy, he fisted his cock so hard he saw stars for a brief moment. "Shit...you know what to do with it. Let me hear you cum."

Andrea didn't need any more encouragement and placed the vibrator against her slick opening first to get it wet, before circling her clit with it lightly. She gradually increased the pressure as she teased her clit, as well as the surrounding areas with vibrations.

Cam heard the change in her breathing right away. Then came the moans, groans and little cries she tried to hold back, as he continued to firmly long-stroke himself. "Don't hold back baby. Don't forget those sweet breasts of mine either. Grab'em, squeeze'em, pinch those nipples for me."

Andrea followed his instructions as she slipped the toy inside herself and turned up the speed dial. "Cam! Cam!"

She was panting in his ear, or maybe he was panting in hers? Hell, Cam didn't know and didn't care. His strokes had turned to short, jerky motions. Right now, he was really thankful that Andrea had insisted on that lotion, otherwise he'd have friction burns out of this world. "That's it baby, I'm so close."

His voice was so guttural that she could barely understand him. "Me too!" She felt herself start to clench around the vibrator before she jerked it out and pressed it directly to the bundle of nerves that made up her clit. "Cam! Oh my god I'm cumming!"

As he heard her release over the phone, he dropped his cell to clench the bedspread, as his own climax took him over. "Hell yes!" He shouted out, loud enough for her to hear. After he spilled all over his fist and stomach, he fell back on the bed, spent literally and figuratively.

He finally found enough strength to pick up the phone again. He still heard her labored breathing and smiled. Seemed like she'd cum as hard as he had. "You okay?"

"I think so." Her heartbeat was slowly coming back down. "That was..."

"Fucking fantastic. I am *very* glad you called."

Now that the heat of the moment was gone, she couldn't believe what had just transpired. Quietly, she said, "I am too."

"I was missing you, you know." When she remained quiet on the other end, he continued. "I'll be home in two days...I can't wait to see you."

"Same. I'll email you tomorrow, okay."

"I hope you can get to sleep now."

Andrea couldn't stop the big smile that creased her face. "I have no doubt I will."

"Goodnight, pretty eyes."

Chapter Fifteen

Andrea was almost lightheaded with excitement! The day after their phone sex episode, she emailed him about coming to her place for dinner once he returned. Now it was Friday and he was on his way back. To prepare for dinner she left work early, picking up last minute grocery items and condoms. She was keeping the meal simple, but she hoped it would be tasty.

Once she got everything mostly done, she took a quick shower and paid extra attention to pampering her skin with smell goods. She chose a flowing fall skirt and a sweater that shaped and enhanced her breasts nicely. Her hair had been washed and dried, then straightened by one of those heated brushes the night before. After bumping the ends, she tucked her hair behind her ears and let it be. After all, she was hoping it would be messed up by the time the night was over. At a quarter to six she started setting everything on the kitchen table, then ran to check her phone. There were no texts from him saying anything had changed, so she expected him to arrive any moment.

Cam was happy to be back in Michigan, even as tired as he was. He'd had to diffuse one of the Director's panic attacks just hours before leaving for the airport. The guy had wanted to add some changes and then insinuated that he doubted Cam would be able to meet the New Year's Eve deadline. Luckily, he had reigned in his temper, when he'd really wanted to say, *"Remember that you chased me down and begged me to take this job."* It was rare that he lost his temper, which was lucky for others. Robert had once told him, he was a scary guy when he let his temper snap.

He ended up arriving to the airport on time, only to find the flight was delayed. He was supposed to touch down at four and have enough time to run home to clean up before heading to Andrea's house at six. The plane was an hour late, and while they made up time in the air, he still touched down close to five. By the time he got his bags and picked up his car, it made sense to head directly to her house. Tired or not, he was looking forward to seeing her. The rest could wait.

He was lucky there was no bad weather, so he arrived just in time. He took his laptop bag in with him, as he didn't want to leave it in the cold car. Of course, he backed up his work on a digital system, but he didn't want to risk it while working on a project this big. He rang the doorbell and Andrea promptly answered it.

"Camden!"

"Hey baby!" He'd barely set his bag down before she was wrapping her arms around him and taking his mouth in a possessive kiss.

When they broke apart, he said, "Now *that* was a perfect way to greet a man."

Grinning, she pulled him through the house by his hand. "Go freshen up if you like. We're eating in the kitchen. Everything is ready."

When Camden came back, they sat down to dinner. He knew she'd said she could cook a bit at Thanksgiving, but this was his first time getting a full meal. As far as he was concerned, she'd outdone herself. They ate spinach-stuffed chicken with crème sauce, sautéed asparagus and baby red potatoes, along with a caesar salad. They spent the leisurely dinner catching up. She asked about his trip and his assignment first. When he got tired of talking about that, he turned the conversation to her.

Eventually, he helped her clear away the table, before following her to the living room, where they sat continuing their conversation. It was one of the things he liked most about her, how they never ran out of things to talk about. She was a sight for his tired eyes for sure. He'd been surprised but pleased by the passionate kiss he'd been given upon arrival. Now, he was feeling more relaxed than he thought possible. Snuggled up on her couch, with the TV on low in the background...he could get used to coming home to this.

The random but truthful thought jarred him, as he half-listened to a story she was telling him. He really *could* picture sharing a home with Andrea, coming home to her each day. Sharing their space, chores, food and time together. The thought felt right. He smiled warily and shook his head. It was hard to deny it, when he'd rushed straight from the airport to her, instead of cancelling. His need to see her had trumped his need to sleep in his own bed...at least if he was alone in it.

"Hey, are you okay?" Andrea had noticed he seemed distracted and tired. Not surprising, as this business trip had been stressful with a deadline looming, not to mention the grueling travel.

"I'm good." He tilted his head and gave her a slow, soft kiss. "Real good, now that I'm back home."

He played with her hair and gave her an intense and searching look, which made Andrea think, *finally!* She had hoped he'd make the first sexual move. Instead, he just continued to stare at her, like he was looking for an answer to a question that hadn't been asked yet.

Cam wanted to tell her what he was thinking...but knew that she wasn't where he was in the relationship. He was determined to get her there, it would just take some time.

With that goal decided, it felt like the stress of the last two weeks hit him all at once. He was sure the two glasses of wine he'd had, didn't help either. He needed to do some more thinking, get his game plan together before he gave her the sales pitch, so to speak. However, he could do all that when he wasn't so mentally out of it. "Sorry, I'm just really beat. I enjoyed everything about dinner. I'll have to repay the favor and cook for you soon."

"It was no problem. I enjoyed cooking for you. After all, you were away working hard."

"I appreciate it. Look, I'm totally exhausted. I'm going to head home and call it a night. Catch up on my sleep."

"Oh!" It had never occurred to her that he would be *so* tired, that sex wouldn't be on his radar. This was not in her "get Cam into bed" plan. She placed a hand on his wrist. "You can sleep here instead of driving home in the snow."

"Snow?"

"Yeah, the forecast said it would start in the late evening. I peeked out the kitchen window after dinner and it had already started."

"I don't know why I'm surprised. I think I got accustomed to Cali weather."

"Yep, you got spoiled." She glided her fingers down to hold his hand. "Will you stay...I don't want you to leave."

"Now, you know I can't seem to deny you. If you don't mind calling it an early night, then I'd appreciate not having to drive in that mess."

"That's fine. You know I'm not a true night owl anyway."

"Okay cool. Let me hit the bathroom."

"Take your time. You know where everything is down here, but let me know if you need anything. Then come on up, my door is the one on the right. Oh, and turn off the lights down here when you done." Andrea waved him away and then rushed upstairs.

She hurriedly stowed away the candles she had strategically placed around the room, as well as tossing the condoms back in a drawer. Romance would have to wait for another night. She had a two-story house that was smaller than Camden's, especially since she didn't have a finished basement as a usable space. However, since she had only two bedrooms, that meant each room had more space. Her master bedroom was large, with a big walk-in closet and a spacious connected bathroom. Camden had never been upstairs, so he wasn't aware of that.

She rushed to brush her own teeth and use the bathroom before replacing her sexy underwear with plain bedclothes. She was wrapping up her hair when he softly knocked on the door before coming in. He looked around before letting his eyes land on her. Then he gave her one of his slow, sensual smiles, though she could plainly see that sleep and not bed sport, was on his mind.

"Get out of those clothes," she said.

"Yes, ma'am."

She rolled her eyes, but gave him a smile over her shoulder as she got into bed. "You'll sleep better if you're more comfortable."

"Right, right...that's exactly what I was thinking," he said, giving her a wink.

She watched him undress down to his underclothes. She found it cute that he took the time to fold his clothes and put them out the way. As he slid in bed, she turned off the light, before giving him a quick sweet kiss. "Goodnight Camden, I'm glad you're back." She snuggled her back up against him. "Get some rest."

Cam settled in, pulling her close. She felt good in his arms...she felt *right*. Giving her neck a kiss, he whispered in her ear, "I'm glad to be home...with you."

Chapter Sixteen

Cam was putting the finishing touches on dinner as he thought about last weekend. Even though they'd gone to bed early, they'd still slept in until nine the next morning. Andrea had insisted on making breakfast instead of going out in the snow, so they'd cooked together. He had wondered if his "realization" would have changed with some rest. The answer had been a firm "no", as they spent the morning and early afternoon together. In fact, being homey with her had solidified the startling understanding that he was falling in love with her. Just the thought made him shake his head. He'd only been in love one other time, but he supposed it had been puppy love, since it was in high school. That, like a lot of things had come to an end with the death of his parents in his senior year.

His parents had only been in their mid-forties when they were killed by a drunk driver, coming home from one of their many date nights. They were good parents to him, caring and active in his life. His father had been a North Carolina transplant to Michigan, which is one of the reasons he'd gone there for college. His mother had been the youngest of four siblings and the outcast of her family.

They'd all had the potential for a good life, but the difference had been his mother's drive. She had been the only one in her immediate family to go to college. Her siblings and some cousins had called her stuck-up for wanting more out of life than having several kids by the time she reached her early twenties. Instead, she'd graduated, got a good job, and met his father not long after. When they got married, they moved to a better neighborhood in Detroit, and that just made the divide even worse. Cam's parents had taught him to be proud of where he was from and where they lived, but had also stressed there was nothing wrong with wanting more and uplifting your community as a whole.

Compared to his cousins, he'd had nicer things and more varied experiences. Though his mother wasn't close to her two sisters and brother, she had tried her best to treat her nieces and nephews right. Needless to say, he ended up having an ambivalent relationship with his cousins because of all the tension between the adults. When his parents passed, he'd actually told the social worker he preferred to stay with a foster family, over his own. He'd known the only reason that either sister had stepped up was the thought of getting the monthly check that came along with him. Even though his parents were only middle class, his Aunts had used his mother for money when she was alive. He wouldn't allow them to do it to her in death as well.

Even though his family home had been paid off a few years before they passed, he knew the court wouldn't allow him to live there without an adult, and he wouldn't turn eighteen until after the school year ended. He spent the rest of the year focused on keeping up his grades through his grief and making plans for the future. Monique, his girlfriend at the time, hadn't understood the swift change in him from teen to grown-up. While she had felt for him, she hadn't really *understood*, and didn't want a boyfriend who had the weight of real adulthood on his shoulders. She, like most of their class, was trying to live it up and put adulthood off for as long as they could.

Both of his parents had life insurance through their work, which he mostly left alone and let the interest build. They had also started a college fund for him when he was born, and it had a modest ninety thousand dollars in it.

He'd had more than enough to support himself that first year in the cheaper state of North Carolina and go to college. It helped that he obtained scholarships as well. In his sophomore year at Duke, he'd made the hard decision to sell his childhood home, as upkeep while being in a different state was too difficult. The money from the sale of the house, plus the insurance, enabled him to get both degrees debt-free, buy his house free and clear, and have a decent cushion while he built his own consulting business. Though his parents had not been present, they'd left him enough tools to build a good life.

Not all of his experience with extended family had been negative. His father's family in North Carolina had welcomed him with open arms. Of course, he'd visited them almost every summer when the family had taken a vacation, but this was different. He grew close to his cousins, and their parents while he was down there. In fact, he'd lived with his family while getting his undergraduate degree to save money. He was also able to forge a bond with his grandfather for a few years before he passed. That had allowed him to see where his father got a lot of his personality from. Living there for six years had taught him what family *could* be. Now, he had finally found someone he could envision having his own family with. He just had to make her share his vision.

Andrea slowly made her way to Camden's place after work. Though it wasn't snowing now, it had snowed a couple of inches yesterday, and there had been flurries earlier too, which made the roads slick and messy. She mentally swatted away her irritation. This was winter in Michigan after all. Glancing at the time on her dash she figured she would still make it by six. His place was really only about fifteen minutes from her office. She'd given herself a full thirty, due to it being rush hour on top of the bad weather. Cam had told her to show up hungry and for the first time he'd had a clothing request.

Today had been her office's annual ugly sweater party. In the three years she'd worked there, she had never participated. However she wasn't trying to wear an ugly sweater for her job this year either, particularly since she was seeing Cam after. Instead, she compromised. She wore jeans like Camden suggested, and a long, semi-sparkly purple sweater, with a matching sparkly scarf. That was as close to a holiday sweater as she got.

She'd told him that he didn't have to cook her a payback dinner, but he'd insisted. He was still working heavily on his current project, with the goal of completion in the next two weeks. She hadn't argued with him, as she'd found he could be stubborn about certain subjects. Besides, who was she to turn down a home-cooked meal? She knew he could cook pretty well and after this hectic week, she'd be happy with whatever he put in front of her. She was just glad that it was the weekend, and she was ready to relax. Something she seemed to do easily enough when around Camden.

When she pulled into his drive, she let out a delighted laugh. He hadn't told her he would be decorating for the holidays. She rarely did. A wreath on her door or a festive sign in her window was the norm for her. She didn't see the point in anything more. But as she looked at his classic green and red Christmas lights and his lighted plastic Santa in the yard, she was suddenly feeling the holiday spirit. She was still smiling when Camden opened the door and swept her inside.

"You made it, got a little worried. You know fools act like they've never driven in snow before."

"Tell me about it. It wasn't so bad, I guess. What's with the lights? I don't know why, but it never occurred to me that you would be the type to decorate."

"You have something against Christmas lights?"

"Actually, I love yours, they just surprised me. Soon as I hit the corner, they were, *bam* right there!"

"Good, they make a statement. Come on in. I hope you're hungry."

"I am! This better be good. I skipped lunch in anticipation of your feast."

"Well that's putting pressure on me. Can't have you disappointed, now can I?"

Dinner was delicious and worth the wait. He'd made one of her favorite dishes, chicken marsala. He'd paired it with garlic parmesan noodles, long green beans, and garden salad. When he brought out his Bailey's pound cake with ice cream for dessert, her eyes got big.

"Hope you don't mind. It's literally the only dessert I know how to make."

"Not at all. I loved it at Thanksgiving! I meant to ask you for the recipe." Andrea was already digging into hers.

"No can do. It's a family recipe. My Mom was a good cook, but a horrible baker. My Dad taught her how to make his favorite dessert, and then she taught me how to make it when I was sixteen."

At the hint of sadness in his voice, that she heard whenever he spoke about his parents, she reached across the table and squeezed his hand. "Well, it's delicious. I'm sure they'd both be glad you're keeping the tradition alive." When he gave her a small, sad smile, she decided to change the subject. "So, why did you want me to wear jeans tonight? The way you just stuffed me with all this food is making them real tight."

Now, a spark of merriment entered his eyes. "No worries. After you finish your cake, we're about to go work it off."

Around another bite, she asked, "What?"

"Don't worry about it. The sooner you finish, the sooner we can go."

She gave him a side-eye, but focused on the rest of her cake. She never outwardly encouraged his need to surprise her, but secretly she hadn't been disappointed yet! She finished up as he cleared the table. When they were both ready and she joined him by the door, he still refused to tell her where they were going. As he helped her into the car, she asked, "You're not going to blindfold me or something?"

"No, but if I ever did, I bet you'd like it. Trust me."

"Mmm-hmm." She let it go, but couldn't help the mental image of being naked and blindfolded that popped in her head. However, he didn't even ask her to close her eyes as they headed downtown. He parked in a lot near Campus Martius Park and they got out to walk to what she hoped was a close destination.

"Okay, now tell me where we're going in this cold." It was nearing 9:00 pm, and was only about twenty-five degrees out.

"We're going ice skating."

"Seriously? Can you skate? I've never been."

"Nope, not a lick."

Andrea laughed incredulously. "So, neither of us knows what we're doing?"

"Exactly. A new experience we get to do together." He smiled and gave her cold lips a quick peck.

They reached the rink not long after and as he paid for their entrance fee and skates, she looked around. Behind one end of the rink stood the sixty-foot Norwegian Spruce Christmas tree that was a staple of downtown. She'd read an article last month when the tree lighting ceremony took place, that it was wrapped in more than nineteen-thousand multi-colored lights and ornaments. The enormous tree was breathtaking up close. That light, fun feeling she'd felt upon seeing his house lights were tripled when she looked at the tree.

"Here you go." He handed her a pair of skates. "Give the man your shoes."

She came out of her musings to give Cam a smile before complying. They sat on a nearby bench and laced up. "Just so you know, I'll be blaming you for every fall."

"You can roller-skate, right?"

"Yeah, I'm pretty decent at that."

"I heard it's the same."

"You *heard*, you don't *know*. I'm still blaming you each time my ass meets the ice," she said good-naturedly.

He helped her stand up and pulled her against his chest, crossing his arms behind her back to cop a feel of the body part she was taking about. "I have zero problem taking care of that ass." He gave her a squeeze and she actually giggled. "I mean, your ass is in capable hands."

He went to give her another squeeze, but she pushed away from him, almost landing on her aforementioned behind. As she righted herself and carefully turned forward, she looked at him over her shoulder. "Try to keep up, Camden." With that she made her first few hesitant steps forward onto the smooth ice.

Luckily, it wasn't overly crowded, although there were enough people for her not to feel as if all eyes were on her. Camden was quickly by her side and they made a slow lap around the open rink. By the second go-round, she was getting the hang of it. While it didn't feel as natural as roller-skating did, she was pleased to find that overall, staying upright wasn't an issue. Annoyingly, Camden seemed to get the hang of it, far quicker than she had. He was already making bigger movements over the ice.

By their fourth go-round, he grabbed her by the arm in spite of the squeal she let out and they began to hesitantly skate in tandem. Soon, she relaxed against his arm as they went around and around, just enjoying the atmosphere. Though the night was cold, it was clear and they could see the stars up above. The lighted tree gave off colors that reflected on the ice. So it seemed as if they skated on a kaleidoscope of colors.

She was thinking about how beautiful it was when Camden switched it up and started skating backwards in front of her. "You just *have* to try and be fancy, huh?"

"That's not it. I just want to look into your eyes."

"You think you are such a charmer, don't you? You're the one with the amazing eyes and you know it."

Cam smiled, pleased that his idea had turned out so well. She had not made one objection to their outing and had jumped in with both feet, literally. "You just don't realize the power your eyes have. Keep looking at me with them and I'll be falling for you in no time."

Andrea grinned. "You gone fall all right, but not because of my eyes."

He went to reply, but at that very moment, a kid of about eight zoomed a little too close behind him, throwing off his balance. Andrea gave him credit, he quickly released her, so she wouldn't go down with him. He hit the ice on his ass, followed by a small slide. She gave herself credit for not laughing at him as he scowled in the direction of the child.

"Sorry!" his assailant called out as he continued in the other direction.

She was smirking as she reached down to help him up.

"How is this fair?" Cam complained. "Who was looking out for *my* ass?"

"It didn't look like you fell that hard."

"Whatever...I think you should kiss it and make it better." He grinned lecherously at her.

"How about this instead?" She put her arms around his neck and stretched up to give him what was supposed to be a quick kiss, but his arms locked tight and the kiss ignited like two dry twigs. Just like that, the sights and sounds faded around them until it was just the two of them. She had no idea how long they stood there, almost in the middle of the rink, in each other's arms.

"Don't forget there are kids out here. Knock it off," a passerby commented.

The message must have penetrated at least one of their brains and they parted ways to watch their breath puff out in the air. Finally, she looked up at him and asked, "Did that make it feel better?"

"It definitely did." He didn't tell her while the ache in his behind had faded, now another of his body parts was throbbing. He tucked a few escaped coils of hair back into her hood before taking her arm again and setting off.

They were quiet as they started going around again, even so Andrea's heartbeat wasn't quite back to normal. She had never been the type to like PDAs, and luckily neither had her partners...that is until she'd met Camden. He was always touching her, no matter where they were. He made it seem so natural and uncontrived that she'd become comfortable with it. She glanced around at the crowd, filled with couples, families and groups of friends having fun, laughing and enjoying the night, just as she was.

She thought over the entire night and sighed happily. Camden was so good to her. First, the wonderful dinner and then the surprise activity. What had he said? *Something new for them to experience together.* He was always creating "firsts" just for the two of them. Going out of his way to do something sweet or thoughtful. She bet so many women complained about their man never planning an outing, while she never had to worry about that with Cam...wait a minute, was she thinking of him as *her man?* At this moment, the actuality didn't really matter. What she realized was that she *wanted* him to be her man. He was hers for the taking, so what the hell was she waiting on?

She really liked Camden. He helped her have fun and made her happy. She could fall for him. She looked up at the clear sky full of winter stars and finally admitted, at least to her own mind, that she *already* had. He had given her another perfect date night, and what had she given him? As they approached the spot where they first got onto the ice, Andrea slowed them down and steered them to the very edge. When Camden looked down at her in confusion, she smiled confidently up at him.

"Take me home." It was time she claimed her man.

Chapter Seventeen

Cam didn't ask questions as they turned their skates in and headed back to the car, though his mind was racing with plenty of them. Did *home* mean *his* house? Or did it mean she was about to go back to hers? After that steaming kiss on the ice, he hadn't been thinking clearly since. He wasn't sure if he was imagining what her smile implied, or not. She kept up light conversation about their time at the rink and he pretended to be engaged, when in reality, he was still trying to figure out what *home* meant. If she meant *his* home did that mean she intended to finish what they'd started in front of a crowd of people? His dick seemed to think they were headed to the bedroom, and he tried to temper its expectations. He didn't have a lot of time to contemplate however, as it didn't take that long to reach the house.

When they arrived, he pulled directly in the drive, as she'd moved her car to the curb before they left. He got out and came around, opening her door. He figured he might as well play it safe. Just like he'd told his dick, nothing was guaranteed at this point.

"I hope you had fun tonight."

"I did! The whole night was wonderful. Thank you for the unique outing. We should do it again."

"My pleasure. You should get out of this cold." There, he'd left it in her hands to do what she would. If it was up to him, they'd be getting warm using skin-to-skin contact.

She reached out and grabbed his gloved hand. "I'm going inside Cam."

Cam...she called him Cam...she was going inside. These were good things. These thoughts jumbled his mind as they entered the house. It was downright embarrassing how nervous she made him. This woman had already been in his bed, yet here he was, as hesitant and horny as a teenager. Then again, Andrea made him feel things no other woman had, which was why she was so dangerous.

Inside, they both wiped off their feet and took off their winter footwear and gear. As he hung up their coats, she tossed her small purse aside carelessly. Andrea was excited to take this next step with him, and was confident in her decision. When he moved to stand beside her, but didn't touch her, her smile dimmed. She hated that the usually assured Camden was so hesitant about their physical relationship now. Then again, he had stated she would need to be blunt for them to be intimate again.

"Do you want anything or-"

She quickly cut him off by placing a finger over his lips. "Just you Cam."

"Are you sure?"

She looked him square in the eyes and placed her palms on his chest. "I'm positive. I can't wait to show you just how sure I am, when we get upstairs."

Finally, she saw a flash of unrestrained desire light up his eyes and curve his full lips. Leaning up, she nipped his chin before hurriedly stepping back and running for the stairs.

"Hurry up Mr. Holden, I think we've both waited long enough." She only made it to the third step before Cam was there, wrapping his hands around her stomach and pressing his lips to the back of her neck. They stumbled up to his bedroom, amid groping hands and kisses.

Cam turned up the lights a bit and pulled her further in the room, shutting the door. Now that he'd gotten the green light, his body was ready to go! But he was enjoying her playful manner, and didn't want to rush their first time together in months. He mentally told his body to settle down before grabbing the scarf around her neck and slowly pulling her towards him.

When she was close enough, he leaned down and gave her a slow, deep kiss, until he felt her go soft in his arms. Instead of backing off, he turned the kiss more aggressive as he let his hands roam down to her waist. He reached the end of her sweater and started pushing it up. He felt her shiver at the first contact, of his fingers on her skin. He ran his fingers lightly up and down her spine, smiling against her mouth, as her legs gave way.

To keep her standing, he sent one hand down to her rump, as his other continued its upward journey to the back of her bra. He managed to unhook it with one hand. When it snapped open, Andrea reared back to catch her breath. He noticed her eyes were starting to glaze over, but not nearly enough. It was time to get skin-to-skin. He pulled the sweater up over her body, then quickly reached to remove his own. By the time his head cleared the collar, he was able to watch her bra fall to the floor.

When he stepped close again, it was Andrea's turn to get her hands on him. His warmth tingled her fingertips, as she gripped his back, their mouths attacking each other. When she felt his hands cover her breasts she moaned, then groaned as he started to roll her nipples between his fingers. God, how her body craved his touch! She started grinding her lower body against his and heard his low chuckle.

Andrea didn't think he knew just how much she wanted him, but he would in the next few minutes. She slid her hands around to his defined abs before she tackled his belt. She wanted him naked, in her hands...in her mouth. She dragged his jeans down his hips, hooking his briefs along the way, before pushing everything to his thighs. She broke their kiss to squat in front of him, then continued removing his clothes. When she got down to his feet she fully kneeled, so she could slide everything off, including his socks.

When she was done, she slid her hands up the backs of his strong calves, then around to the inside of his muscled thighs, until he parted his stance. She could hear the change in his breathing already, and her lips curved into a naughty grin of her own. When she moved one hand to cup his balls, she heard him inhale deeply. She lifted herself on the balls of her feet until she could run her tongue up the underside of his penis. She *slowly* licked all the way to the tip. She did it again, starting from the base, her tongue moving along the thick, pulsing vein. She intended to take him in her mouth during the next pass, only to feel his hands pushing at her shoulders.

Andrea firmed her grip around him possessively. She viewed him through her lashes with an actual scowl on her face. "I want to."

He loosened her grip and dragged her up. "I got you, don't I always give you want you want?" he whispered, wrapping her in his arms.

"But I want-"

He cut her off by taking her mouth and shifted them until she was facing the bed. There was no way in hell he would last long enough to get inside her, if she gave him head right now. Just looking at her on her knees licking up his shaft, had almost done him in. When he thought she was sufficiently distracted, he pushed her onto the end of the bed, kneeling down to remove her socks. By the time he was finished, Andrea was already trying to wiggle her jeans and panties down over her curvy hips. He started tugging them from the bottom to help.

Once her clothes were out the way, he joined her on the bed. Rolling onto his back, he pulled her on top of him. When she started kissing down his body, he didn't stop her. Instead, he said "Baby turn the other way for me."

Andrea's mind was on her goal, which was below his waist. She turned slightly annoyed and confused eyes his way.

He just smiled and shook his head. "Come sit on my face...just backwards, so we both can have what we want."

When what he was suggesting finally clicked, she quickly moved her body over his, until her head was over his straining penis. She didn't waste much time looking, before she dipped her head and *finally* took him in her mouth. She sighed as her lips wrapped around him tightly, giving that first tentative pull.

Cam groaned before distracting himself with her sweet wetness. He parted her folds and ran his tongue down the center before curling it to dip lightly inside. He started kissing, sucking, and licking her pussy in earnest as the first taste of her entered his system. It was like his body had been missing a vital supplement, and now that he had it, he wondered how he'd gone without it for so long.

Andrea had never had sex in the sixty-nine position before, however she was sure it wouldn't be the last time. Since concentrating on her task was impossible with his talented tongue driving her crazy, she just let instinct kick in. She loved that they could give each other pleasure at the same time. The more he gave to her, the hungrier she became...for his cock, *in* her mouth, *against* her tongue. She stroked and squeezed him, then licked and sucked him, fondling his balls in her palms, making both of them moan.

Every time she moaned around him, he felt it along his entire length. This woman was going to drive him insane. With one hand, he rummaged in his bedside drawer for a condom. He needed to be inside her now! He gave one more long lick to her pussy, before slapping her ass smartly. When she looked back and saw what he held in his hand, she swiped it from his fingers and put it on herself. He smiled shamelessly as he watched her sheath him in protective latex. When she was done, she returned the smile.

Pulling her up across his chest, all smiles were gone, as he tangled his hands in her wild curls for a frenzied kiss. He rolled until he was above her, parting her thighs with his knee. As he began to push forward, they broke off the kiss to look into each other's eyes. Cam felt something *tighten* in his chest as he slid *home* inside her.

Andrea felt something *loosen* in hers as their bodies connected again. She spread her legs wider wanting him closer, needing him to be a part of her. Clutching him by the hips, trapping him with her thighs, she felt him begin to move in long, slow thrusts. She was already so sensitive and primed from his tonguing. Her nerve endings were already on fire, her heart rate racing quickly.

Cam stayed low, wanting as much of their bodies to touch as possible. Each time he stroked forward, he brushed her clit, making her tighten around him, until he withdrew and did it all over again. He rained kisses along her neck and shoulders, wanting her to know how precious a gift it was to be with her. But he also wanted her to know she was his. That there was no going back this time, no escaping what was between them. He slipped his forearms beneath her shoulders, so he could lock her in place for his bucking hips. Then he increased his speed, and the power behind each thrust.

Andrea cried out as Cam picked up the pace. She dug her nails into his back, lifting her legs to fully wrap around his waist. She wanted everything he had to give! She loved the feel of him pounding into her, the friction against her clit made her want to scream. So much so, she buried her face in his neck and bit down on his shoulder. He responded with a growl that sent an instinctive shiver through her whole body. His hand snaked into her hair, pulling her head back roughly so he could claim her mouth in a fierce kiss.

Cam was so close. When she had wrapped her legs around him, it had given him a deeper angle. When her inner muscles started to spam around him, it triggered the start of his own release. He bit her lip hard enough to make her lust-clouded eyes open. He wanted them in this together as they went over the edge. Gazing at one another, they soon both cried out in sexual bliss, their climax rocking both their bodies at once.

When it was over, he let the rest of his weight drop down onto her, trying to catch his breath. A few seconds later he tried to move, only to have her legs wrap tighter around him. So tight he felt small ripples of aftershock move through her. She finally released him so he could dispose of the condom. He returned to bed, pulling her to his side, tucking her head in the crook of his neck. He waited until her breathing went back to normal and her fingers made lazy patterns on his stomach before speaking.

"Are you okay?" They both knew he wasn't talking physically.

Andrea tilted her head up, a dreamy satisfied smile playing on her lips, before draping a leg over him possessively. "I'm fantastic."

"You don't have a sudden urge to go home right?"

"No, but I *do* have a pressing need to do it again." She reached out and grabbed his manhood. "That is, if you think you're *up* to it."

That startled a laugh out of him. He quickly rolled on top of her. "My buddy may have to catch up, but I can think of some things to get us started."

Chapter Eighteen

Andrea smothered a yawn as she drove down the highway. Even though she only had another hour of her drive to go, she hadn't quite woken up yet. Of course, she blamed Camden. Yesterday, during their Wednesday lunch date he had convinced her to stay the night with him before hitting the highway. She'd agreed of course, wanting another night in his bed. After all, she would be gone for the long Christmas weekend. As she continued to drive, she thought back on the last five days.

After the second time they'd went at each other on Friday night, they'd fallen asleep and hadn't gotten out of bed until almost noon on Saturday. Since it was lunchtime, they'd eaten leftovers from the night before. Afterwards, he'd hauled up a fake Christmas tree from the basement with boxes of ornaments, along with various tree trimmings. They had sat around in nothing but robes, decorating. He mentioned it was the first tree he'd helped decorate since he's parent's death. That led him to telling her funny stories about his childhood and she'd shared some of her own as well.

A playful fight with tinsel, ended with them having sex in front of the tree. The rest of Saturday had been spent alternating between doing nothing and more fooling around. Sunday, when he'd woken up with a morning hard-on, she'd been more than happy to take care of it. She was sore in all the best places! He'd given her a massage that ended up being more for his benefit than hers, before they finally settled down. Rounding out the majority of that day watching movies and talking.

At around eight o'clock that night, she'd made noise about needing to go home because of work the next day. They'd had sex one last time, with her bent over the end of the couch, before she headed out. When she'd finally gotten home, all she'd wanted was a proper soak in the tub. Since she was afraid of falling asleep and drowning herself, she'd settled for a hotter-than-normal shower instead. They hadn't seen each other until their lunch date three days later.

She had never been a sex-crazed woman. Sex was usually nice for her, but had never left her craving it. She had always been able to take it or leave it. But with Camden, the flood gates had been opened and she seemed to want him all the time. Which was why she'd gone home on after work, loaded up her luggage and headed to his house for more intoxicating lovemaking.

She'd been caught off-guard by what else she'd gotten from him. They had been naked on his bed when he'd reached over into his nightstand, where she'd assumed he was getting a condom from his never-ending supply. Instead, he'd pulled out a jewelry box.

"*Cam you didn't!*"

"*I did.*" When she just looked at him, he continued. "*Aren't you going to take it?*"

"*I can't take a gift from you.*"

"*You don't even know what it is yet.*"

"*Whatever it is, I can't accept it. You didn't have to get me anything because we're...you know.*" She nodded to the bed.

"*Baby you good in the sheets, but I got this for you when I was in California before the holidays. I meant to give it to you last weekend.*" He tweaked one of her nipples and grinned at her. "*However, I had other distractions.*

Come on, Andrea take the gift, it's the season of giving after all."

She had reluctantly opened the slim gold box to reveal a cable wrapped amethyst stone, with a ring of tiny diamonds on a sterling silver chain.   "Oh, Cam it's beautiful!" Before she could say anything else, he was putting it around her neck and fastening the lobster clasp. She went to speak, and he shook his head.

"Just say thank you."

"Thank you. It's so lovely."

"I'm glad you like it. When I saw the color, I thought of you." He caressed the jewel dangling right above her breasts.

"I feel bad. I didn't get you anything."

"I can think of something you can give me right now."

That had been the end of that conversation, or at least the verbal kind.   Andrea couldn't believe he'd bought her something for the holiday. Sure, she had accepted a few gifts in her previous long-term relationships. Her last boyfriend had gotten her diamond earrings for their six-month anniversary. Which was partially why, when the one-year mark hit, she'd been expecting a ring of the engagement variety, and had been sorely disappointed. She shook off that unpleasant memory and focused on how good it would be to see her parents.

She had grown up happy, in a middle-class neighborhood, with lovely parents.   Cincinnati could be either a nicely blended city, or a very racist one. Strangely, she was thankful for the rough edges she'd had to learn to navigate early. They'd served her well through college and throughout her career as a black woman who needed to be taken seriously. Being a Change Management Consultant at PWC was no easy feat. She made a living telling mainly rich, high-level white men and women what they were doing wrong within their company. She had thick skin, and had to use it on a fairly regular basis.

She attributed a lot of her strength to her mother. Who to put it plainly, didn't take shit from anyone. Oh, she never *started* anything, but she sure would *finish* it. Bernadette Cole was a freedom fighter and womanist rolled into one. Conversely she was also one of the nicest people you would ever meet, fun, loving and outgoing. Her mother had taught her right from wrong, and how to fight for the right when no one else would. She knew how to stand her ground when adversary came knocking. Now her father, was mostly the opposite of her mom. He was forever calm and easygoing. Oh, he could be a little serious at times, which is where she got that side of her personality from, but he was the perfect balance to her mother's feistier persona. They were definitely an opposites-attract story, but they made it work. They had planned well and provided for her *and* their own early semi-retirement. Now, they were able to enjoy their late-fifties by relaxing and waiting on her to pop out a grandkid. Andrea gave a little chuckle at that last thought as she made the final turn into their driveway. She was home!

"Bernadette, stop squeezing that girl so tight before you cut off her circulation."

"Earl, you know you'll be doing the same thing in a moment. Our only baby is home!" Bernadette sometimes wished it had been medically possible for her to have more kids. Not a *lot* more, but at least one other. However, Andrea was a blessing, one that she would always be grateful for.

"You right. Hand me my baby girl!" Andrea was passed to her father, who was sporting a truly ugly Christmas sweater. It was an odd tradition that her father did each year which annoyed her mother. Though she never technically said anything, there was a good bet it would disappear after this weekend, forcing him to buy a new sweater next year. Her mother took her coat and her dad grabbed her bags.

"Are you hungry?"

"I could eat." She'd left Camden's house at seven in the morning, and had only paused long enough to hit a drive-thru for some coffee.

"Then follow me to the kitchen and I'll whip up some lunch for us. We didn't eat, as we weren't sure what time to expect you."

"Sorry about that. I wasn't sure this time around when I'd be hitting the road." Usually, Andrea called them the night before with her plans. Instead she'd forgotten, and called them this morning when she got on the road.

"It's fine, your mother just worries about all the idiots driving during the holidays. I'll go set your things in your room. Go catch up with your mother. Make sure she gives me extra meat, whatever she makes."

The house she grew up in was a ranch-style house with a partially finished basement. The main floor housed three bedrooms, one of which had always been the guest room, slash her mother's craft room. Andrea had urged her mother to dedicate that room strictly for her projects and make her old bedroom the official guest room. Her mother wouldn't hear of it. Insisting her only child would always have "a room" in their home. As such, Andrea always returned home to a bedroom that still held touches of her high school and college days.

Now, she sat at the kitchen counter watching her mother pull out the makings for a sandwich, salad, and some frozen sweet potato fries. She was happy to see her mother using the air fryer she'd gotten them last year. Andrea went to work on her father's sandwich so she could sneak him that extra helping he wanted.

Her mother saw what she was doing over her shoulder and just rolled her eyes, then took a good look at her daughter. She looked relaxed, if a bit tired, but good overall.

"So, tell me, how are you doing? Everything okay? Didn't get a call from you last Sunday."

It was not unheard of, but it was rare for her to forget to call. She hadn't thought of them once while rolling around with Cam. "I'm sorry, Mama, I was just really busy. Everything is good, really good."

"Hmm, okay. Pretty necklace you have on! Is that something new you bought yourself for the holiday?"

"No..." Should she lie...what for? Then again, it was her mother who had taught her not to take gifts from boys, least they want something back in return. However, her mother was probably the least stuffy person in this house. At the end of the day, she wouldn't care. "A friend gave it to me for Christmas."

"Oh, that was nice of Mika." Bernadette knew damn well Mika hadn't given her that necklace. If she had, Andrea would have just said so.

"Not Mika...another friend of mine."

Bernadette resisted rolling her eyes again as she turned over the fries in the fryer, then went to work on the salads. Her daughter could drive her crazy with the way she would circle around a subject before giving information. "Does this friend have a name?"

"Cam, I mean Camden Holden."

Bernadette gave her a pointed look over the salad bowls before asking, "Is he black?"

"You sound like Mika."

"There's a reason I like that girl. So, answer the question."

"Yes, he's black."

"Just checking. With his name, especially the last name, it could have went either way. Anyway, that's a really pretty necklace. I see it's your favorite color too. Are those real diamonds?"

"Yeah, I think so."

"Hmm...how long you two been dating? Why is this the first time I'm hearing about him?"

"Oh, about four months. It's not serious...I mean it wasn't at first...I don't know why he never came up."

"I see." Bernadette let the kitchen lapse into silence as she read between the lines of what her daughter didn't say. She figured it was serious, which was why she hadn't heard about this man. Besides, men who *weren't* serious didn't buy necklaces with real diamonds, in a woman's favorite color after only four months. She was starting to get a pretty good idea of why her daughter hadn't called her last Sunday. Biting her lip to keep from smiling, Bernadette thought it was about damn time! It had been forever since she'd heard Andrea even mention a causal date. She was happy to know there was a man who'd gotten under her daughter's skin.

"Tell me a little bit about him before we go eat with your father."

"He's thirty, he'll be thirty-one next July. He has his own successful web design and development company. He owns his own home. No kids or marriages under his belt."

"Okay, all of that sounds good! Now tell me, is he cute?"

"Mama! Yes, he's really handsome actually. He's really nice, funny even. He somehow finds a way to make me relax." Andrea kinda forgot her mother was there as she waxed on about Camden. "He's really sweet and thoughtful, always thinking of something fun or different for us to do." Her hand went to the necklace. "He's always giving me treats or gifts, like flowers, and this necklace. I tell him to stop, but he does it anyway."

Bernadette took the fries out before commenting, "Sounds like you're in love with him."

Her mother's statement snapped her mind back to reality. "What! Why would you say that?"

"Honey, if you saw the look on your face when you were just talking about him, you'd say it too."

Andrea actually jumped up off the stool and started putting the food on trays. "I would not! We barely know each other! It hasn't even been six months! I just started slee..." She managed to cut herself off. Her mother didn't need to know about their sexual habits. "I don't think we're at that point yet."

Bernadette reached out, covering Andrea's hand to stop her nervous movements. "Honey...look and listen to me for a quick moment. I know you're cautious with relationships, especially after the last one, but love doesn't work on any schedule you have. You should have learned that after Damon. Four months or four years, it doesn't matter. If you are in love, then you're in love. I don't want you to miss out on something good and real because you think it hasn't been enough time yet."

Then Bernadette laughed, before turning to finish plating up the food. "If you've found a man that puts that dreamy look in your eyes, treats you right, and gives you love bites that make you forget to call your mama, then you should keep him! This man sounds like a good one. I know I hope he is, because I believe he has your heart."

"I...don't know about love yet. I just know he makes me feel good on every level. I like being with him. We're friends."

"Friends is a wonderful place to start." She gave Andrea a reassuring smile and let the subject drop. Her baby was stubborn and would see things in her own time, lord willing. "Now, let's go feed your Daddy before he comes storming in here."

The long weekend went by quickly as she spent quality time with her family. When Christmas rolled around that Friday, they exchanged gifts after breakfast. They went to visit some extended family during the day, and finished the evening with a relaxing dinner. That night, she texted various friends and co-workers to wish them a merry Christmas. She called Cam and had a brief conversation with him as well.

On Saturday in the late evening, she joined her father in the small, heated shed he had built in the backyard. It was where he did all his wood crafting. It was a skill that had been passed down in his family. Her great-great-great-grandfather had brought the skill from Tennessee when he'd made the trek up from the South. Her father made small-to-medium wood items mostly. He sold his items at markets and local fairs or gave them away as gifts. It was a hobby, that he just happened to be very good at.

"Hey, Daddy, can I watch a little?"

"You can watch and even help. Take that stack of snake wood and cut it, into six-inch parts for me."

Andrea had been taught how to use the table saw as a young teen. Putting on protective gear, she went about doing the task she'd been given. They worked in comfortable silence for about ten minutes, until she brought the finished pile of wood to his work table.

"What are you making, anyway?"

"Got a custom order from one of the ladies your mother knows. She wants some custom doll tables for her twin granddaughter's birthday next month."

"That's going to be nice!"

"I think so. I'm glad you came out here. I wanted to talk to you, if you don't mind."

"Sure, what's up?" She leaned back against a shelf, waiting on her father to continue.

"Your mother told me about your young man." Earl held up his hand to stop whatever Andrea was about to say. "From what I heard, he sounds like he has the potential to be a winner. She thinks you may have already fallen for him."

"Mama talks too much and doesn't know what she's talking about."

"Now, we both know whether we like it or not, you mother is usually right. Talk to me. Do you love this Camden?"

"I don't know," she mumbled sullenly. Right about now, she wished she'd left that necklace in the box.

"Does he love you?"

"I don't know that either. I mean apparently, I'm a horrible judge of character when it comes to how men act when they're in love. I thought Damon was in love with me and I was absolutely wrong."

"We're not talking about him." Earl's voice went tight. He didn't like to think about the man who had broken his baby's heart. "We're talking about this new guy."

"I feel like it's early in the relationship to be talking about love, Daddy. He treats me great, so zero complaints on that score. He seems to like me just the way I am and has taken time to get to know me. I think he cares for me." Her father said nothing, just waited for more. Reluctantly, she told him about Thanksgiving. "He...invited me to spend Thanksgiving with him and the people he considers his family."

"Ah well, that's something. You *both* could be falling in love. Would that be fair to say?"

Andrea breathed easier at the way her father phrased it. "Yes, that would be fair. I'm hoping what we have continues to grow."

"In that case baby girl, I hope it does too." Earl stopped what he was doing and turned fully to face her. "Let me say this last thing and then I'll be done. If you do find love, or love finds you...fight for it. Until I met your mother, I'd never met a woman I wanted to fight for. Oh, there were those I wanted to 'win the game' with, but none that I wanted to fight for when things got hard. If something tries to keep you from that love, whether it be other people, him, or even yourself, fight for it! Fighting for your mother is still the best thing that I ever did."

Andrea gave her dad a hug. "It's sweet that you still love mom so much. I promise when I find real love I'll take your advice."

"Good, and one more thing. Once you figure out your mother was right...bring that man down here to meet us."

Chapter Nineteen

The last two months had been a whirlwind for Andrea. Her relationship with Camden had continued to progress along positive lines. They continued to have great conversations and outings, often followed by sex...amazing and splendid sex. With the winter weather, she had quickly ended up keeping clothing and other basic items at his house. She hadn't purposely started leaving stuff. It was just easier to go to his house after work since it was closer than hers, so she often did. She had expected him to be put out of sorts by the slow accumulation, but he hadn't said a word. Then one day, she found all her hair and bathroom knick-knacks sitting in a pretty purple basket on his bathroom counter.

Now, here they were in February and the dreaded V-day was upon them. Usually, for Valentine's Day, she and Mika would get together if neither of them had a date. A few of those years had included a small group of other ladies. This year they both had dates, as Mika had started dating someone back in January. Meanwhile, she found herself driving to meet Cam at the Whitney downtown. The holiday fell on a Sunday but he was able to secure them a table the Friday before. She was excited to see him, as they'd been super busy this week, and hadn't spent as much time together as they would have liked. This was the most excited she'd been about the commercial holiday in years!

Cam was pleased as he waited for Andrea to arrive. He'd had to plan early and pay a premium on top of that, to secure a private booth in a secluded corner of the restaurant. He'd lied to Andrea about having a meeting far away as an excuse for them to both drive separately. He knew his woman well and after they talked about what was on his mind, she might feel like she needed some space. This way, if she wanted to go to her house instead of his it would be less awkward.

Robert had tried to get him to share his plans for tonight, but all he admitted to was a romantic dinner. Cam planned to tell her he loved her, before the night was over. He'd tell the rest to Robert, depending on how she reacted to his declaration. He had been ready to say the words since right before Christmas. But he hadn't wanted her to think he was just saying it because they were having sex again, or any other "excuse" she might have not to believe him.

If it was up to him everyone would know. He'd waited his whole adult life to feel this way about a woman. Now that he did, he didn't care who knew...well assuming she felt the same way about him. He stood up when he noticed the maître d' walking her over to his table. She was wearing a clingy, deep red, long-sleeved dress that barely hit her knees. Black leather high-heeled boots that went up *just* enough for her dress to brush the tops. He watched as a few men eyed her as she strolled by. They could look all they wanted. She was his, and he planned to keep it that way.

They ate dinner and drank expensive wine, while they talked and laughed in their private alcove. As they were finishing dessert, he pulled out a silver and red gift box from the inside pocket of his suit. "Happy Valentine's Day, baby."

"You have to stop giving me gifts."

"You keep saying that, yet I keep doing it. Open it."

Andrea sighed with what she admitted to herself, was fake exasperation and opened the round De Beers jewelry box. Inside was a ruby and diamond tennis bracelet. "My god Camden, I can't accept this! This had to be too expensive."

Cam knew she really wasn't into things that cost a lot of money. He'd noticed she had some name brand clothes and a few bags, but it wasn't her normal habit to buy expensive things, which was another reason he enjoyed her as a person. She made more than enough money to afford high-end brands, but more often than not, she chose to focus on other things. Which was also exactly why he loved spoiling her.

"Do you like it? It matches your outfit." He helped fasten it around her wrist.

"I love it. It's beautiful and I can tell it's the real deal. You can't give me stuff like this."

He still held her hand, and now he squeezed it, to get her to look at him instead of the bracelet. "What law says I can't buy my woman gifts?"

"Oh, I'm your woman, am I?"

"Yeah, you are. Look, I wanted to talk to you about us tonight. I think it's time we made this thing with us official and exclusive." When she just stared at him, he chuckled, more amused than worried. "Look, did I say that right? I have to be honest, I've never had this conversation as a true adult. Let me know if I'm messing it up."

Andrea smiled back at him and relaxed, though she wanted to probe his last comment some more. "What do you mean? I thought you said you've had a couple of serious relationships."

"I have. Honestly though, those were when I was much younger. Back when you don't have these kinds of direct conversations, it's just assumed after a while. After I finished my Master's, I focused on getting my business on solid ground. There have been women of course. When they brought up being serious...well I was never on the same page, and things usually ended."

She hadn't expected to hear that. Strangely, as much as they talked about any and everything, they had steered clear of the details of their past relationships. "Don't you think it's weird that we haven't talked in-depth about old relationships?"

"Baby, you barely wanted to go out with me. I had no desire to bring up our past, so all the things you don't like about men would be foremost in your brain."

"Was I that bad?" Andrea grinned.

"Well, you remember how we finally got our first date right?"

"I do...I remember how it ended as well."

"I do too. I really should be buying Mika some jewelry."

Andrea gave a small snort of laughter. "She would *so* take it without blinking." Looking down at the gorgeous bracelet, she asked, "So, why were you never feeling the other women you dated in the last few years, enough to make it official?"

Cam sat back and took a sip of wine before he answered. "I think it was a combination of things. When you hustling to get name recognition, you have less time for women on all levels. I was also getting settled with the house. It took me and Robert almost half a year to get things to where they needed to be. I mean, I guess if I'm being honest, at the time, I sought out women who at least at first, didn't want anything serious. We were just spending time together. Most of the relationships fizzled out on their own after a few months. I had a couple that made it to around six months. When being in a truly committed relationship was brought up, I had to be truthful and let them know I wasn't thinking long-term at the time."

"I see," Andrea said quietly.

"What about you? Tell me a little bit more about the last serious relationship you had. The one you said didn't end well a few years back."

Andrea took a *big* gulp of her wine. This was exactly why she hadn't pressed to have this conversation before either. "His name was Damon. We met when I was working on a project at his company. He flirted, but I put him off until the project was done. I guess I was flattered that he pursued me after the fact, so we started dating. Three months turned into six, and next thing you know we were reaching a year of what I *thought* was a serious relationship. I thought we were headed to the next level. He thought we made a good couple, but wasn't thinking forever."

"Did he cheat?" Cam asked soberly.

With an agitated shrug, Andrea answered, "I don't know. Not that I was aware of. Looking back, I can say we didn't spend as much time together as you would expect for a couple together that long. We were circling around the perimeter of each other's lives. I mean we went out...on the weekends and for special events. We didn't connect as much during our daily lives. I guess we didn't really know each other."

Cam reached for her hand again. "Like we do."

"Yes, like we do. Tell me what makes you feel differently about me, than the other women who wanted you for their man?"

"So you *do* want me to be your man," he said playfully.

"Answer the question, Mr. Holden."

"Fine. While I felt comfortable with them and we were having fun, I never felt I needed them, if that makes sense. I didn't miss them when I went on trips. I didn't need to talk to them every day. Didn't need to hear their voice to get a good night's sleep. That's what makes you different. I not only *want* you in my life, I *need* you in it." He leaned forward as he felt her hand tremble under his. "How do you feel, Andrea? I need to know."

"I feel the same. It's crazy how we've tangled our lives together so fast, but I can't imagine you not in mine at this point. On the way over here, I was thinking about how much time we spend together, and how it doesn't annoy me. It scares me sometimes. But, when I think about it...I don't want to change anything. I love spending time with you...being with you." Andrea damned her mother's intuition. "I love you...period."

Cam didn't let her get another word out as he crushed his mouth to hers. The rounded booth allowed them to get hip-to-hip, and before she knew it, he had her almost in his lap. That was until they both heard someone discreetly clearing their throat.

"Is there anything else I can get you?" Their waiter asked.

"Yeah, the check," Cam told him with a big smile on his face. He reached for his wallet and pulled out a credit card. "Here, take this and take care of the bill."

"In a rush all of a sudden?" Andrea asked as the man walked away.

"Hell yes. You just told me you love me. I want to get you home, so you can prove it. I can't believe you said it first. I was going to tell *you* today, whether you wanted to hear it or not."

"Well, I technically haven't heard you tell me that you do."

He touched his forehead to hers. "Andrea Renee Cole, yeah that's right, I know your middle name. I've been falling in love with you for the longest. I love you and I'm thrilled that you love me too."

It was her turn to grin like an idiot, as she gave him a quick kiss before leaning back. "I'm relieved to hear that we're on the same page."

"Your receipt, sir." The waiter slid his card onto the table and discreetly left.

"Not so fast," she said, as Cam hurried to sign the slip and leave a tip. "I guess if you can give your woman gifts, then I can give my man something too." She reached inside her purse, pulled out a medium sized wrapped box and shyly handed it over to him. She wasn't accustomed to getting men gifts and she was worried he wouldn't like it.

"I feel like it's my birthday or something. I'm getting *I love you's* and gifts." Cam unwrapped the box, wondering what in the world she could have gotten him. He saw the familiar blue box and couldn't believe it. "You got me some Campfire Audio earbuds!"

"I hope you like them. I remembered the name of the brand you talked about when you were complaining how horrible your current ones are. I couldn't remember the exact style, so I picked the color I liked. I think those are the Polaris."

"Baby, these are great! Top of the line, but you really shouldn't have spent so much on some earbuds."

"It's okay, I'm good. Plus, I know how listening to music helps you work. You needed something of quality." Many times when they hung out, one or both of them would have to work, and Camden used his music to block out everything as he worked on his complex web designs. She'd wanted to get him something he could use.

"These are perfect. Thank you." He pulled her up and led her from the booth. "Let's get out of here. I want to go reenact the ending to our first date. Remind me to pick up a little something for Mika."

"Umm, I don't think your woman is cool with you giving gifts to another chick."

Cam grinned. "I like the sound of that...my woman."

Chapter Twenty

The middle of April found Andrea headed back to her parents' house, only this time Camden was driving. She normally visited this time of year for her mother's birthday. Naturally she had stumbled over asking him to come. Luckily, he'd gotten the gist of what she was trying to say and had been excited to meet her family. In fact, he'd been a little more excited than seemed normal. Most men would have been a little apprehensive about meeting their girlfriend's parents. Now they were minutes from arriving before he finally showed any nervousness.

"So, is your daddy going to meet me at the door with a shotgun?"

"No, though I do believe he knows how to shoot. Matter of fact, so do I."

He took his eyes off the road for a quick second, giving her a look of surprise. "Really?"

"Yep. Mika convinced me to take a women's only CPL class, a few years back. She ended up hating it, but I really enjoyed myself. I go to the range several times a year."

"That's hot, my baby packing heat."

"I'm not packing!" For some reason, the thought had her cracking up. "I'm just licensed to do so."

"I still find it hot. You should take me to the range and teach me how to shoot for my birthday."

"Deal." Andrea had told him to ditch the GPS once they got off the highway. "Turn left at this next street. Go down one block, turn right, then you'll be on Baker Street."

They arrived as her father was walking to the front of the house from his shed, waving at them as they parked. Her father opened the front door and shouted that the "kids" had arrived. It was a warm day for early spring, so she didn't freeze while standing outside giving her daddy a hug. She waited until her mother arrived before making introductions.

"Camden, this is Earl and Bernadette Cole. Mama, Daddy this is Camden Holden."

Bernadette studied the man who had an arm around her daughter's waist. The pictures she had badgered Andrea into sending, didn't do him justice. She waited to shake his hand and was happy when he gave her a firm grip. She gave him a small smile in return.

"It's great to meet you in person. However, let's all go in the house. It's nice out, but not that nice." She pulled Andrea forward and said over her shoulder, "Earl, help that young man with their bags."

The two men watched the women disappear into the house before walking the few steps back to the car.

"You need any help?" Earl asked.

"No sir. We didn't bring much." Cam reached into the backseat, picking up their two small carry-on bags. They were only staying Saturday night, then leaving mid-day on Sunday.

"That's what I figured. My wife just wanted Andrea to herself. I gotta warn you, we're pretty possessive of our baby girl."

"I don't blame you sir," Cam said as he made it through the door. "I seem to have that same feeling when it comes to Andrea."

Andrea was feeling a sense of déjà vu as she found herself in the kitchen making lunch once again, while her mother questioned her.

"He is quite handsome."

"You knew that Mama, from the pictures you made me send."

"I was just trying to make sure he was black. That's why I wanted those pictures."

"What is wrong with you?" She ruined her scolding by laughing. "I told you last time he was black."

"I just had to make sure. You can be secretive from time to time. I'd love any grandbabies, but I did have my heart set on some cute little brown ones."

"You are crazy, and there will be no talk of babies. No one is having any. No time soon at least."

"Mmm-hmm." Bernadette wasn't going to argue the point. "What's that flashing on your wrist?"

Andrea slid up her sleeve to uncover the bracelet. She twisted her wrist this way and that way to show it off. "Camden gave it to me on Valentine's Day." Quietly, she added, "I told him I loved him."

"Was that before or after he gave you all those diamonds and rubies?"

"After, but what difference does that make?" Andrea frowned, not liking what her mother was implying.

"Depends. Did you say it because of the gift? Did you say it because it was Valentine Day? Or did you say it because you meant it?"

"Of course I said it because I meant it. I don't go around telling men I love them just because of a gift or a stupid holiday."

Bernadette was reassured by Andrea's outrage. She wanted to make sure her baby was moving forward, for all the right reasons. "I'm glad that's the case, but you need lower your voice while talking to me."

"Sorry."

"I get it, and I'm happy you've fallen in love *and* had the nerve to tell him. That part can be frightening. I'm proud of you."

"It was scary, but I'm glad I did. It felt right."

"Well, I'm excited to see where this goes. I'm look forward to getting to know him."

"I honestly think you and Daddy will like him. But enough about me. I'm here for your birthday!"

Bernadette waved her away. "It's no big deal."

"It is! Don't forget I'm taking you to dinner tonight."

"You don't have to do that. It's just another year that I'm thankful for. I'm hoping for many more, now that I got a shot of getting grandbabies."

Her parents spent the morning talking Cam's ear off *and* embarrassing her. Showing him her old pictures and art projects. Later that evening her mother got her wish, and they didn't go out. Instead, Andrea insisted that she and Cam would cook for the family. After a quick run to the grocery store, they made a pleasing meal, topped off with a store bought birthday cake. Then spent a quiet evening talking and watching a few movies that everyone could agree on.

"Well we're turning in. You kids can stay up if you want," Bernadette said at ten o'clock.

Cam stood up, stretching, "No. I forgot how much a road trip can take out of you. I'm more used to a quick plane ride."

"You put him in the guest room right?" Andrea asked.

"I sure did," Earl spoke up, before patting Cam on the back. "We're a relaxed household...but not *that* relaxed."

"Daddy, seriously?"

"No worries, Mr. Cole. I'm on my best behavior."

"Yeah, that's what men always say, what they *do* is another matter. Didn't I tell you to call me Earl?"

"Sure thing, Mr. Cole," Cam said flashing Andrea a grin.

As Andrea settled down for the night, she thought about how well the day had gone. Like most things, Camden had made meeting her family feel easy and comfortable. The total opposite of when she had brought Damon here. Cam had answered all of her mother's inquires, never once showing irritation. He'd gotten along with her father, discussing education and various other topics. Her father had even volunteered to show Cam his workshop in the morning before they left. Andrea was very pleased with the outcome of the day. In fact, she was downright giddy about it. So much in fact, that she felt like celebrating. Which is how she found herself sneaking into Camden's room forty-five minutes after they'd turned in.

"Mrs. Cole, I know it's your birthday and all, but you need to get *that* kind of gift from your husband," Cam muttered as the door opened.

"You know what...that is not funny. My mother would *never*." Andrea was choking on her laughter, as she went to turn on the small nightlight under her mother's work desk.

"Hey, you never know. Some families are into some kinky stuff. Your mom does look good for her age but I didn't get the vibe that your father was down for sharing."

"You are stupid." He sat up over the side of the bed, and she straddled his lap, her knees on either side of him. "But since you've brought up kinky..."

Cam took the kiss she gave, as he ran his hands over her hips. "What are you doing in here? You were there when I told your father I was going to be on my best behavior."

"I sure was. I never said *I* would be."

Cam's penis went from semi-hard to rock steady at that statement. "Come on, Andrea. I'm not having sex in your parents' house. I'm trying to make a good impression here."

"You have! That's why I'm here. I want to celebrate how well today went." She moved her hand between them, massaging him through his pajama bottoms.

"We are *not* doing this...no matter how bad I might want you. Your parents are close by. Plus, I didn't bring any condoms with me."

"They're not *that* close. One thing I liked as a teenager was that the master bedroom was at the other end of the house. I could always sulk in peace."

"Yeah...but condoms." It was getting harder for Cam to remember why they shouldn't do this, as more and more blood traveled down south.

"I never said we'd need any. I want to reward *you* for making such a good impression." She kissed him again before sliding off his lap. There was enough light in the room for her to cross to the craft cabinet and open it. She quickly selected a short length of satin ribbon that her mother often used and came back to the bed. "Sit back and relax." Andrea said, before dropping to her knees between his.

"You can't-" That was all he got out before she pulled him out of his pj's and put her mouth on him. Lord, he really hoped there were no guns on the premises.

Andrea got him good and wet before wrapping the satin around him. She concentrated on sucking the first few inches of him while she stroked the rest with the smooth material. She smiled around him as she heard him groan. The night was definitely going to have a happy ending.

Cam had slept like a baby after Andrea had crept back to her room. Since they'd resumed the physical side of their relationship, he was constantly shocked by how sexually free she was.

Once breakfast was over, he found himself following her dad outside to look at his workshop. He hoped to god he

154

could keep his mind from drifting back to last night while he talked to the man. Mr. Cole showed him around and explained a few of the projects he was working on. He had zero experience with woodworking and asked some questions about the different machinery.

As they were finishing up, he asked. "Andrea said you built this yourself?"

"Yeah, not that she would really remember. Her mother finally let me get started on it when she turned five. Money and time were tight before that, with a toddler running around."

Cam couldn't help but grin. "Was Andrea a handful at that age?" He could just picture a little brown girl causing mischief and pouting when she was caught. Even with just the one day spent with her family, it was clear Andrea had been loved and spoiled as an only child.

Earl chuckled and shook his head. "She was, but then most young kids are. She was inquisitive. Always wanted to know how something worked, why it worked, what it was for. Full of questions, even after she got older. Probably what makes her so good at that job of hers. Drove her mother crazy. Me, not so much. You'll learn when you have your own kids. Things that would normally annoy you, won't."

Cam had to clear his throat first before he voiced his next thought. "Speaking of..."

When Camden trailed off, Earl raised his brow and tried to help the young man out. "Speaking of what? Don't get tongue tied now. You were doing pretty good. If you got something to say, say it."

"Speaking of having a family of my own one day, I'd like to have a family with your daughter. I'd like to ask your permission to marry Andrea."

"Well, I wasn't expecting that! We're not that traditional. Oddly enough, my wife grew up in a more religious family, and they had some strict expectations of how one should behave. Drove her crazy, as she's always been a free spirit. It's what attracted me to her, that shine and energy she had. I suppose I appreciate the gesture, but the only permission you should be worried about getting is Andrea's. If my baby girl wants you, then so be it. Do you think she's on the same page as you? Have you talked about marriage? About where you see your future going?"

Cam frowned. No, they hadn't had those conversations. But he knew what *he* wanted, and what he wanted was Andrea. "Well no, we haven't. I guess I just wanted to meet you guys and let my intentions be known."

Earl couldn't help it, he laughed in the young man's face. "Again, I'm the wrong person you should be sharing your 'intentions' with. I like you, even more I like how you treat my daughter and how happy she seems with you. I think you have some more talking to do...with Andrea. I wish you good luck with that."

Chapter Twenty-One

Her birthday was the last day in June, and it fell on a Saturday, which worked out perfectly for her. Mika and a small group of girlfriends had taken her out to dinner Friday, and tonight she was spending with Camden. She had told him it wasn't a big deal, that they could just stay at home relaxing. She was only turning twenty-nine, not the dirty thirty. As this birthday rolled around, Andrea was extremely satisfied with where her life was at.

She would never have imagined being this happy and most of that was due to Camden. Her life was fuller with him in it. What they had, worked. He may not have known it but he was the best birthday present she could wish for. After much debate, they had reached a compromise. A simple dinner would be followed by chilling at her place, doing whatever she wanted. She was looking forward to curling up on the couch and just relaxing with her man.

When they had left the visit from Cincinnati, Cam had to admit her father made some good points. They hadn't talked about children or a number of other important topics. Like how they managed their finances, or even their general goals for the next few years. So, he'd started asking her questions during the drive back and ever since. He snuck them in whenever he could. He found out she admired her parents' marriage and hoped to have a strong one herself in the future.

When he asked her if she ever regretted being an only child, they had both talked about their experience growing up and agreed that having more than one child wouldn't be a bad thing. Her father had been right. He needed to know more details of what his life together with Andrea might look like. None of what he had found out, changed his mind about having her in his life long-term. They may not have known every little thing about each other, but there would be plenty of time to learn once they were engaged and then married.

He had taken her to a low-key birthday dinner and now as they entered her home, he was both excited and nervous. The next few minutes would change the rest of his life. He would have preferred to do a big and extravagant wedding proposal, but he had to remember it wasn't all about him. His end goal was getting the girl, and that meant giving her a proposal that would be meaningful to her. He snapped out of his thoughts, when she called his name for the second time.

"Camden, I was asking did you want anything to drink? I'm dying for some water. I don't think I had enough between last night's alcohol fest and the heat of the last few days."

They were standing in the archway between the kitchen and living room as she waited on him to respond. He could actually use some water, as his throat was dry as a bone and his palms were actually sweating. Wiping them off on his pants, he took her hand and led her towards the couch.

"Can we just talk for a moment?"

"Camden, I told you no gifts and I mean it!" Andrea shook her head as she settled on the couch. When he hadn't whipped out a gift at dinner she thought for once, he had listened to her. "I don't need anything. Dinner and just being with you is enough. I just want to zone out tonight. I promise I'll let you do something exciting next year for the big 3-0."

"That's kind of what I want to talk about." When she gave him a questioning look, he continued, "Just hear me out for a few minutes."

"I'm all ears. Though you may want to hurry before I die from dehydration."

He smiled before taking her hand in his. He liked her dry since of humor. "Give me two minutes. Then I promise the birthday girl can have whatever she wants."

She made a motion of zipping her lips and smiled at him.

Taking a deep breath, he went for it. "I want to start by saying I've enjoyed these ten months getting to know you. I'm glad that when you talk about your birthday next year, you still see me in your life, which is exactly where I want to be. I know it may seem fast, but what I know for sure is I love you. I want us to be together for many more birthdays, holidays, the good and bad days to come." He reached in his pants pocket and took out a ring box.

"Andrea Renee Cole, will you marry me, so we can spend the rest of our lives making memories together?"

Andrea hated when people used clichés like *time stood still*. But now, she understood that one well. Time paused as her brain struggled to comprehend what he had just said...what he had just *asked*...what he was *holding* in his hand. The ring looked to be a one carat diamond with two purple diamonds on each side. My god are there even such things as purple diamonds? Her mind was all over the place and only came back when she heard him say her name.

"Andrea?"

"Cam..."

"You called me Cam, so that's a good thing right?" He joked anxiously. He had expected some shock, of the happy variety. Not prolonged silence and the slow look of dismay that was creeping onto her face. "Say something baby. Don't leave me hanging."

"I don't know what to say."

"Say you'll marry me."

Andrea finally looked up and focused on his face. She couldn't do this. She scooted back and stood up. "I can't...I can't marry you."

He sat back. Disbelief at her utter refusal clear on his face. With a loud snap, he closed the ring box. "I don't understand what you mean by *can't*...don't you at least want to talk about this? I know I may have caught you off guard-"

"I mean we can't get married. I'm sorry, but we just can't." Andrea had never been prone to theatrics in her life. She was the level-headed friend, the cool and calm co-worker, the dutiful daughter. But right now, she didn't know if she was coming or going.

Cam stood up, trying to hang on to his temper. She'd said no. What he needed to do, was try and be rational and find out why. But all he *wanted* to do was smash something. "Andrea, you're not making sense. Look I thought this would be the perfect time to ask, apparently I was wrong. But it's okay. I get it. You need some time to think about it."

"Cam, it's ridiculous that you even asked. I mean we barely know each other!"

"Ridiculous? It's been almost a year. Plus, I know all I need to know. I want to spend the rest of my life with you."

"Well, I don't know enough! I mean this is too fast. You...we can't make a decision that will affect the rest of our lives out the blue."

He stalked closer to her and she backed up, which really pissed him off. "This isn't an *out of the blue* decision for me. I've thought long and hard about this for months. *Months* Andrea! Are you telling me you haven't thought once, *just once* about us getting married? Even as we talked about kids and finances? Did you think I was just making conversation?"

"Yes! That's exactly what I thought!" Andrea turned from him and started to pace back and forth. "I didn't think you were talking about *us*, just in general. Just in passing. I mean come on, Cam. We haven't talked about where we would live or how we would truly combine our lives. We haven't planned anything!"

"Damn a plan, Andrea! Not everything needs a chart or timeframe. I assumed, *wrongly*, after you said yes to my proposal, we could talk about all those things. Plan after. But you won't even consider it."

"There's nothing to consider right now. We can't get married or engaged. We don't even really know each other!"

"You looking me in the face and saying that? We've spent every moment possible together for almost the entire last ten months. We've talked, we've laughed, and we've shared our secrets. Talked about our dreams for the future. Now, you're telling me you don't think we know each other? You have to be fucking kidding me!"

"You're taking it the wrong way!"

"How exactly should I take it? When the woman I thought loved me-"

"I *do* love you!"

"Do you really? Because it's not sounding like it. You sitting up here, telling me that basically the last ten months of our lives haven't meant anything. They didn't matter. That what we have isn't *good enough* to build a foundation on."

"I don't feel that way. Please Cam, listen. I'm just saying...that I don't think this is the right time to get engaged. I do love you, but I don't think we're ready yet. There is so much that needs to be worked out. Maybe in another six months or so, we can reconsider this. I just think we need to slow down."

"Fuck slowing down again! I'm done waiting around for you to figure out how you feel. I've made compromises, adjusted to give you what you wanted, what you needed. I have needs and wants of my own. I want a woman who loves me as much as I love her, that needs me and wants me in her life like I need her. I want a woman who isn't waiting for the stars to align on some unknown date before she's willing to commit to me!"

Cam was squeezing the ring box in his fist as he invaded her personal space again. "We're not kids, Andrea. I'm at a point in my life where I know what I want when I see it. I want you. I love you. I don't need every small detail mapped out for me, before I can decide that you're a good thing in my life. I don't need to date for two point five years before getting engaged. I *know* in my heart I want to marry you. That if you had agreed to marry me, I would have spent the rest of my life trying to make you happy."

He paused to see if she had anything to say. When she just stood there looking at him dejectedly, Cam was through. He backed away, resisting the urge to shake some sense into her. "I'm done being the one to bend Andrea."

"Wait...what does that mean?"

"Exactly what you think it does. I'm done. I love you. I want to be with you, but I'm done begging for you to meet me halfway. You need to figure out what *you* want. You need to figure out if you think we're worth it. I think we are, but the choice is not mine alone."

"Cam I'm so sorry. I didn't mean to hurt you."

"Well, you did. I'm tired of pulling punches with you Andrea. You know where I stand in this relationship. You can decide once and for all if you're in or out," Cam said exhaustedly. He couldn't take any more of this. He needed to leave. He sat the ring box on her coffee table.

"You can't...I can't keep that...you said we're done," Andrea choked out.

"Damn it Andrea, don't you get it! I don't care about a fucking ring, I care about you and me!"

"I care about you too!" She took a few steps towards him. "Don't go like this."

"Why not? Apparently, there's no future for me here." He turned and started walking toward the door.

She followed quickly on his heels. The reality that he was walking out...potentially *out of her life*, was setting in. "Cam, wait a minute. I love you!"

He turned back to face her as he stood with one foot out the door. "Not enough, Andrea...not enough."

Chapter Twenty-Two

Cam's head was pounding as he slammed out of Andrea's house and back to his car. What the hell had just happened? He revved out of the driveway and forced himself to calm down. Just because his world was crashing around him, didn't mean he had to ruin someone else's by causing an accident.

For a split second, he thought about jumping on the highway and heading out to Roberts place, but scratched that idea almost as quickly as he had it. He didn't trust himself to be around anyone right now. How could he have been so wrong in thinking she was ready to move forward? Tonight made him question if she even loved him at all? Had he been the one with the inflated expectations?

He had done everything in his power to show her how much he cared, virtually from the moment he met her. What else did she want him to do to prove himself? He didn't know, and right this moment he didn't care. He'd meant what he said. He would not be the one going back, waiting for the relationship crumbs that she doled out to him, on some timetable known only to her. She had to figure out if she wanted him in her life or not. He loved her to distraction, but he wouldn't let her make a fool out of him or his emotions.

Mika was at home, chilling in light summer sweats, while working on a campaign in her office. Usually, when she brought home work on the weekends, she did it during the day, so she could keep her nights free. However this

Saturday, she found herself with no date, no function and no best friend to hang with. It was a rarity for her to have zero on her plate during a weekend night, but she was okay with it. Even *she* needed some downtime now and then. However, she was having a brain freeze with the current concept she was working on and figured she was due a break. She picked up her phone and texted Andrea, although she didn't expect to get a response back.

Mika: Did he get you a gift for your birthday? He better have gotten you a gift!

Since she ended her last "hookup-ship" a few months ago, she figured she might as well live vicariously through someone who actually *had* a romantic life. Here it was barely nine o'clock, and she was doing work like a modern day old maid. She couldn't believe how she and her best friend's roles had changed in less than a year. So, it surprised the heck out of her when the phone pinged. She snatched it back up and took a look.

Andrea: Yes
Mika: Shouldn't you be having sex instead of texting me? But since you not what did he get you?
Andrea: An engagement ring

Mika blinked at her phone screen for a moment. Before texting back with shaking fingers, like *she* had just gotten engaged.

Mika: OMG, OMG OMG!!!!!
Andrea: I...said no

Again, Mika did a double take at the screen. What the hell? She wasn't on drugs, but she *had* to be hallucinating.

Mika: I'm calling

The phone was answered before the first ring could finish.

"What happened? Are you okay?" Mika asked the pointless question, as she could hear Andrea crying.

"He...I...I think it's over."

"Wait, wait, wait! Do you want me to come over?"

"No...yes...I don't know! I don't know anything right now."

"I'm coming over. Give me forty-five minutes tops." Mika said before hanging up. Jumping out her office chair, snatching up her laptop as she went, she wasted no time. She went to her bedroom and quickly threw her computer and some overnight clothes in a bag. She was staying the night, no matter what Andrea said. Moving to the kitchen, she grabbed a couple bottles of wine, on the off chance Andrea was running low.

She also went in her hall closet and added a couple boxes of Kleenex. She had a feeling those would be needed more than the wine. Andrea and Cam made an almost sickening couple. What in the world could have caused this mishap on what should have been a night of celebration? Finished, Mika locked up her house and started the thirty minute drive to comfort her friend.

Andrea spent the time waiting on Mika trying to calm herself down. She'd texted Cam that she was sorry and asked if they could talk about this later once they were both calmer. She tried calling him, and it went right to voicemail. That was almost thirty-five minutes ago and she'd gotten no response. True he might not be home yet...but he had in-dash texting and calling. Maybe he really was done, just like he'd said.

She wiped her eyes and then flopped onto the couch, only to jump back up a short time later as she heard the doorbell ring. She almost tripped over her bare feet rushing to the door. Maybe it was Cam, maybe he'd come back! When she opened the door and saw Mika, she deflated.

"Oh...hey."

"I'm sorry." Mika stepped in and gave Andrea a long, tight hug. "Just me. Let's go sit so you can tell me what happened."

Mika settled her on the couch and went into the kitchen. She put the wine she had brought in the fridge and then poured two big red party cups full of Andrea's already chilled stock. This was not a wine glass kind of occasion.

"I don't want anything to drink," Andrea said, when Mika tried to hand her a cup.

"Drink a bit, it will calm your nerves. I could see you shaking from the kitchen."

Andrea started to argue, then just did as she was told. Maybe a drink would help. So far, nothing else had. She took a couple of big gulps and Mika nodded her head in approval.

"Good...now, tell me what in the world happened?"

"I don't know! I ruined everything!"

"Give me the cliff notes, from the top."

"We were back from dinner. He said he wanted to talk, then he proposed. Pulled out a ring!"

"Then...you said...no?" Mika drew out the sentence, because that was the part she was having trouble understanding. Cam proposing was something she'd seen coming. Apparently, Andrea was the only one caught by surprise.

"Yes." Sighing dejectedly, Andrea closed her eyes and tilted her head down.

"Why?" Mika was honestly confused. She had never seen Andrea so taken with a man before. When she had found out Andrea had been the first to say, "I love you", Mika had almost fallen out of her chair. Now her friend was saying "no" to a marriage proposal, that should have had them making wedding plans.

"I freaked out. I just kept repeating like an idiot that I couldn't marry him."

"I assume he didn't take that well."

Andrea's face crumpled and a fresh wave of sobs ensued.

"I'm so stupid. I shouldn't have said that." Mika gathered her friend up, patting her on the back. "I'm sorry. I'm sorry!"

It took a few minutes for Andrea to calm down enough to speak. "He wasn't upset...not at first. Like always, he was his usual understanding self. He tried to reason with me. He said he understood if I needed time to think about it. I screamed at him there was nothing to think about and kept denying even the possibility of us getting married."

"I don't...I mean, why don't you want to marry him? I thought you loved each other and things were going *really* well?"

"I *do* love him...so much." Andrea looked up at Mika, imploring her to believe it. Since she hadn't had any luck convincing Cam of the fact. "I just don't know if marriage is a *right now* thing for us."

"Well...where did you envision your relationship going? You guys have been together close to a year. If you continued to date, didn't you consider a future with him?"

"I...wasn't trying to think ahead, or make assumptions like I did before. I was enjoying our relationship one day at a time."

"Do you want to marry him...someday?"

"I don't know! I just know I want him in my life. I didn't want him to walk out that door and never come back!"

"He'll come back, don't think like that."

"He won't. He told me he won't. For the first time ever, I saw him angry. Worst of all, he was hurt. Sad and hurt because of me. He said he was done waiting on me to figure out what I wanted. When I saw that ring..." Andrea gestured to the box still on the table. "I just kinda blanked out. I couldn't think. I couldn't articulate what I was feeling. I've texted and called him a few times since talking to you. He hasn't answered or responded. I think he's done with me."

"Hold up, he left the ring with you? That's a good sign! If he was really done, he would have taken it. No man pissed about being turned down, is going to leave the ring." Mika snatched up the box, snapping it open only for her mouth to drop. "He bought you *this*?"

"It's beautiful," Andrea said mournfully.

"It's fucking expensive! Do you know how rare purple diamonds are?"

Andrea knew that Mika had real experience with precious jewels. Besides, knowing Cam he had probably spared no expense. He insisted on spoiling her.

"The darker the purple, the more expensive. Purple is so rare! He had to spend at *least* twenty to thirty thousand on this. At least!"

"No!" Andrea snatched the box from her. "Maybe the purple diamonds are fake?"

"I'm not an expert, but I don't think so. It's a beautiful and expensive ring."

"Why would he spend so much on a ring?" Andrea asked, openly confused.

Mika smiled wistfully. "Because he loves you, he thinks you're worth it. Give him some time to calm down. He'll be back."

Chapter Twenty-Three

Robert threw his suit jacket on the back of the car seat before making his way to Cam's house. It was the middle of July, and hot as hell. He hadn't seen Camden in two weeks. The guy had been brushing him off ever since he'd broken up with his girl. Every time he texted him, he only got short messages back, while his calls were sent straight to voicemail. After he hadn't shown up two Fridays in a row, that had been the last straw. Robert figured he needed to check on his friend.

Pulling up to the house, he parked and got out. He rang the bell and got no answer. After trying a second time with no response, Robert decided to go the old-fashioned route and started banging on the door. That earned a response, as he soon heard footsteps pounding closer.

"Who the hell is pounding on my door like the police!" Cam yelled as he jerked open the front door. When he saw that it was Robert, he just stared for a few seconds before asking, "What are you doing here?"

"Checking up on you apparently." When Cam just continued to stand there, Robert shook his head in irritation. "You gone let me in or continue blocking the door?"

Cam moved out the way, but didn't offer any words of welcome as they made their way inside. He didn't offer Robert a seat either, but that didn't stop his friend from taking one. Cam watched as his friend took a slow look around the place and then at him. He didn't care what conclusions Robert came up with. He'd been holed up in his house, being alternatively pissed and depressed. His last big project had ended right before his disaster of a proposal. He had some small ones he was working on now, but those took less mental energy and had more flexible deadlines. Which left him with plenty of time to sulk.

Robert had taken stock of Cam and his place. The house was noticeably messy, compared to how it was normally kept. While Robert was a true neat freak, Camden had always kept his house in order, after all neither of them were young bachelors. How would it look for a grown ass man to have a nasty ass house? Luckily, Cam wasn't near that point...yet. What concerned him more than the house was the man himself. He had a beard growing in, and it didn't look like he'd showered, at least not today. Camden was dressed in a baggy tee-shirt and sweats, as if he had no intention of leaving the house anytime soon. At least it didn't seem like he was drinking...much.

"You didn't show up today."

"I texted you I'd try to make it. Didn't say I would," Cam said nonchalantly.

"Hey man, I know you really liked her, but this is getting ridiculous." Robert didn't have a lot of patience for bullshit so figured he'd cut to the chase. "I mean, ya'll will probably make up or something. You can't go locking yourself away like it's the end of the world over a simple breakup."

"I proposed," Cam said flatly, flopping down on the couch. "She said no. Does that sound simple to you?"

In one of the rare times in his adult life, Robert was left speechless. It was by will power alone that he kept his mouth shut, so something unwise wouldn't come out. He needed to focus on the crisis at hand instead of asking the numerous questions he had.

"Hmm, that's what Eric was talking about at the office."

"Eric?" Cam screwed up his face in concentration. "The guy who handles my accounts?"

"Yeah. A couple of months ago, he was asking me if you were planning a big purchase. I told him to mind his business. That it wasn't our job to share our clients' money activities."

"Nosy bastard." Cam rubbed a hand distractedly over his face. "Remind me if I forget to transfer my account to you."

"I thought we agreed not to mix personal business that way?"

"Fuck it. If I got to have a noisy bastard looking into my business, it might as well be you."

Robert let out a small smile. "I got you." Robert let silence descend upon the room for a while. Finally, he asked, "What happened? It couldn't have been the ring."

"I have no damn clue. I brought her home from dinner, gave a speech like you suppose to, and asked her to marry me. She said she couldn't."

"Did she say why?"

"Naw, not really. Some bullshit about us not knowing each other enough."

Robert wanted to say he thought her assessment made sense to him. The two hadn't known each other even a year. While he had realized that the relationship was serious *way* before he thought Cam understood the fact, he still didn't understand what the rush was. Could you really know someone that fast? Enough to connect your life to them for what was supposed to be forever? Whatever his thoughts were on the matter, he was smart enough to keep them to himself.

"Well...at least she didn't say she didn't love you. Sounds like she just wants more time."

"More time for what?" Cam exploded off the couch and started pacing. "We're not kids. We're at an age where we should know who we are. What we want. She either wants me or she doesn't."

"This is a big deal Cam...marriage. Maybe she just wants to slow things down a bit."

"If I hear *slow it down* one more damn time! Our whole relationship has been 'slow', as far as I'm concerned. I knew I wanted to marry her, share our lives together, back in December. I'm tired of waiting!" His admission seemed to drain his anger, and he dropped back down to his seat.

"Damn bro, that's deep. I could see she wasn't like the rest right away, but I had no clue you were falling *that* fast."

Cam looked at his friend, his face drawn in serious lines. "Man, some of the clichés are true. When it's the right one, you just know."

"If you say so. I think I'd still be running background checks after ten months with my lady."

They shared a grin before Cam shook his head. "No, you wouldn't. When you meet her it will all click into place. You'll see. The shit just comes out of the blue and knocks the crap out of you."

"Who would have thought you'd be the first of us to fall? I'm happy for you though."

Cam lost his smile fast. "For what? This love shit is sucking at the moment. I fell for a woman who doesn't feel for me what I feel for her. I've given her everything she's asked for. I did everything her way, took the relationship at her pace, yet all she could say was we couldn't get married."

"I believe you. I know you give your all when you want something. Have you ever considered though, that just because you go for what you want full-throttle, that other people don't work that way? Maybe she wanted to move in together and see if you guys could work on that level first. Is that so unreasonable?"

"Hell, Robert. You know we *were* practically living together. How many times did you text or call me in the last few months and she was at my house, or I was at hers?"

"*Practically* isn't the same as *actually* living together. Maybe she couldn't see it as clearly."

"I'm not sure she saw it at all. I don't even think she *thought* about us and marriage. In fact, she told me she never had."

"Did she end it? Did she say it was over between you two?"

"No, I did," Cam said, his voice taking on a hard edge.

That statement made Robert sit up straight. "*You?* So, because she doesn't want to get married right now, you gone throw your whole relationship away? How does that make sense? Didn't you just say you knew she was *the one* for you, six months ago?"

"I'm done being the only one trying to move forward in this relationship. Until she can figure out what she wants...which *should* be me. So yeah, as of right now, I'm out."

Hearing the finality in Cam's voice, Robert nodded his head. He knew Cam well enough not to try and talk sense into him at this point. "Okay, let me say this last thing. Don't let pride make you walk out on the woman, who made you have dreams of turning this house into a home."

"I'm not going to her...not his time." Cam shook his head decisively.

"Whatever you think will work. Just know you can be a stubborn bastard."

"So are you. That's why we get along so well."

"This is true." Robert stood up. "Come on, get your grungy ass up and get me a drink. I'll help you clean up this mess. Seeing all this clutter has my OCD acting up."

Mika was wrong. He didn't come back, he didn't call, he didn't text, and he didn't email. All attempts she'd made to contact him in the two weeks since her birthday had gone unanswered. She'd left brief messages, but what she really wanted to say, she didn't want to leave on a voicemail. She didn't know what else to do! She knew he wanted her to accept the proposal, to say that she would marry him. But at this point, it would be misleading.

In the weeks since the split, she'd done what apparently Camden had been doing for months. She thought about their future and the idea of marriage to him. Just the idea put a flutter in her stomach, and she admitted she felt excited at the thought. She *would* like to marry Cam...someday. The thought of accepting his proposal *now* though, made her stomach flutter with fear and anxiety. If only she could make him see she wasn't rejecting him...or them. She just wanted to be sure they were doing the right thing, at the right time.

Chapter Twenty-Four

Andrea sat in her office looking absently at the wall. She really should be working. She wouldn't have as much time tomorrow on Saturday to work, as she had an outing with the girls. Today was Camden's birthday, July 22nd, not that it mattered. It didn't take a special day to have him on her mind constantly. She had mailed him a voucher for an hour at the gun range...for two. She knew he'd received them yesterday, as she had tracking on the envelope. Nothing. This morning she had sent him a text wishing him a happy birthday and that she missed him. Now it was three in the afternoon, and still no word from him.

It was going on the third week after their breakup, and he hadn't said one word to her. She had ducked and dodged her weekly calls to her parents. Sending them texts and emails instead, claiming that she was extremely busy. She didn't have much confidence in holding off her mother much longer. She was so deep in her thoughts that she didn't hear the light knock before her door opened.

"Andrea, can I have a moment? Andrea?"

"Oh, I didn't hear you. Come on in, Michael." Michael Simmons had been her boss since she had joined the company. Rarely did he come into her office for an unscheduled meeting. They were both usually too busy for idle chitchat. She watched him warily as he shut the door and took a seat. She wasn't in the mood to hear about any problems or issues today. Frankly, she just didn't care.

"I wanted to check in with you. Are you okay?"

Andrea frowned and started tapping her pen against her desk. "Of course I am. What made you ask that?"

"You've been distracted lately. Edgy." To make his point, he indicated her tapping.

"Well, I have a lot going on with work, but nothing I can't handle."

"Exactly. You always have a lot going on. We have high-stress jobs and I've rarely seen you let it get you down, especially not for long periods of time. You've been different lately. I've noticed, and so have others."

Andrea sat up straighter and looked him directly in the eye, while trying to keep her tone from being sharp. "Michael, are you insinuating that my work is not up to par?"

"Not at all. As usual, your work is excellent. What I'm saying is you seem off, not like yourself, and it's noticeable. Look, are you having personal issues?"

"If I were, they would be personal now wouldn't they?"

"Andrea, you are a valued member of this firm. I hope in the three years you've worked for us, we've shown you that. You have a lot of folks here that care about you. I'm one of them. Life happens, I get it. But I wanted you to know, whatever is going on it's showing. It *will* eventually affect your work and your interaction with clients. Don't let it get to that point. If you need time off we can make it happen. You have plenty of time to take off."

"I don't need time off," she said tightly.

Now Michael stood up. "Okay. Tell you what, take the rest of the day off. It's Friday after all."

"I have a lot of work to get done."

"It wasn't a request. Go home Andrea. If you really need to work, take it with you. Don't forget we have that strategy meeting Monday afternoon."

Andrea fought the urge to hurl her pen at the door as he closed it. The hell with it. He was right, so she couldn't even be that pissed at him. She needed to get her shit together one way or the other. This is why she avoided relationships. Eventually, there was emotional drama and it wormed its way into all parts of your life.

On Saturday, she and Mika spent the afternoon with the girls at the DIA. The Detroit Institute of Arts was hosting a free Chinese art exhibit and cultural program. Sadly, even though these girls lived in the city, not a single one had been to the building before. They wanted to expose the girls to as many different things as possible. Letting them know the world was a bigger place than just their hometown. Afterwards, she and Mika sat having dinner, enjoying the warm summer day.

"I had a good time with the girls today."

"I could tell. It was nice to see a real smile on your face. It's been a while," Mika commented.

"Yeah, the girls help. Besides, I was told by my boss yesterday that I needed an attitude adjustment." She spent the next few minutes telling Mika about Michael's visit to her office as they waited to order dessert.

"Well...you *are* pretty miserable. You've even lost some weight, which I hate you for. I stress eat and blow up."

"Gee, thanks for pointing out all those *positive* things. I don't want to be miserable, but I don't know how to fix it."

"He still giving you the silent treatment?"

"Yes! I wished him happy birthday yesterday and sent him a gift. Nothing."

"Girl, you need to talk to him in person. It's the only way you'll get him to listen."

"I know, though I still haven't figured out exactly what to say."

"It's been three weeks Andrea...you better figure something out."

They were interrupted as a waitress arrived at their table.

"I'm sorry for the wait. Your other waitress had to leave due to an emergency. I'll be helping you. Did you want to order dessert?"

Andrea looked up and did a double take. It was the blonde waitress from all those months ago who had flirted with Cam. That was the first time she'd felt possessive of him. Thought of him as hers...and now he was gone. Tears stung her eyes and she turned away.

Mika noticed Andrea's reaction, even though she had zero clue to the cause. "Umm no, we're good." She quickly rummaged through her purse for a debit card. "Here, put the bill on this. We may just sit for a while talking though, so no rush." The waitress took it and hurried off. No doubt she was in a hurry to cover her own tables as well as her co-worker's. "What just happened Andrea?"

"I'm sorry. I hate feeling this way! I didn't really pay attention earlier, but this is where we had our first date. Got me thinking about that night...I miss him so much!"

"Of course you miss him. You love him. Tell that man you'll marry him and tell him why you didn't say yes at first."

"I told him why."

"No you didn't." Mika cut her off. "You made up excuses. You didn't tell him you were afraid."

"I'm...why would I be afraid?"

Mika gave her a grim look and said, "Damon."

"What does he have to do with this?"

"Exactly. Nothing. Cam isn't Damon, but you're treating him like he is. Cam isn't going to leave you when things get serious. Cam wants to marry you, Damon didn't. Cam loves you, Damon never did." Mika held up her hand as Andrea went to speak. "More importantly, you never loved him either. He hurt your pride, but your heart was never his to break."

"How can you say I wasn't in love with him? I spent a whole year of my life with that man!"

"Oh please! Look at how you were with Cam, then compare it to Damon. Even a blind person can see that with one man you were just spending time, but you were building memories with the other. Ugh...I sound so mushy, but it's true. You keep waiting on Cam to disappoint you like Damon did."

"I just think Camden is moving too fast, that he doesn't really understand what he's rushing into. I think he'll regret things down the road."

"The man doesn't seem like the foolish, impulsive type to me. I don't think he'd be where he is in life, if that was the case. You have to figure out if he's worth taking a risk for. You do risk analysis for a living. Do one for your relationship this time. Put your head *and* your heart in the equation. Then let the cards fall where they may. If you don't patch this up...I think *you'll* be the only one with regrets."

Saturday night found Robert, a couple of his cousins and Camden hanging out at Centaur Bar and Lounge. They were trying to show Cam a good time for his birthday, which had just passed. So far, the only people having fun were Dev and Darrell. Robert was stuck watching the once typically smiling and easygoing Cam actually scowl at women who were trying to give him some play.

When he wasn't doing that, he was looking at his phone and looking even more pissed. Robert didn't know what to do for his friend, as he hadn't dealt with this much angst since Brihanna was a teenager. Shit, this was exactly why he never got with women that rocked his boat anywhere but the bedroom. He only wanted a body to warm his bed when he had an itch and someone on his arm when he needed a date. He had never pictured himself as a "forever" type of guy. There were just too many unknowns in a deep relationship.

Watching Cam was putting *him* in a bad mood, that even alcohol couldn't fix. When he saw Cam pull out his phone again to glare at the screen, Robert plucked it out his hand.

"Man what the hell!"

Robert ignored his protest and saw that it was a text from Andrea dated yesterday, wishing Cam a happy birthday and saying she missed him. There were no return messages. That was all he had time to see before Cam was snatching the phone back and standing up. "I need some air."

Robert gave him a few minutes, then made sure one of his cousins knew they were stepping out and followed. He found him standing against the side of the building, looking like he wanted to knock someone out. Robert stood in front of him and asked, "Do we need to take this to the ring?"

"Man, fuck off."

"Why didn't you text her back?"

Cam gave a jerky shrug and stared off into the distance.

"She's reaching out and you're still being an asshole? Thought you said you were in love with her?"

"I don't want her well wishes or her gifts."

"Oh, you got a gift too? So, you slapping all *kinds* of olive branches aside. Sounds smart. Have you communicated with her at *all* since *you* walked out?"

"No, but you don't get it. I don't want platitudes. I want her to say we can move forward and get married."

"Ahh, I get it now. You don't want her back unless she gives you exactly what you want, in exactly the way you want. This is the first time since I've known you that a woman hasn't fallen in line with the plans you hatched. It's clear she doesn't want this to be over. I'm sure you're not the only one with pride. You let this go on much longer, ignoring her and she might just take you at your word *and* actions and be done with *you*."

"She needs to figure out what she wants."

"I think it's clear she wants you. Just a word of advice. If you still love her and want her back in your life, end this standoff. If not, it's a fair bet you will lose her for good."

Chapter Twenty-Five

As August rolled in, Andrea gave up on trying to get Camden to respond. She put her energy into figuring out how *she* felt and what *she* wanted in life. Her life seemed very empty without him. She had lost not just a lover but a friend as well. He was her go to person, the one she texted in the middle of the day if something irritated her. He had been the one to bring her soup and medicine when she'd gotten sick in late January. His special talent had been putting a smile on her face when she didn't even know she needed one.

He had always innately gotten her, similar to her mother, who knew something was wrong and would no longer be put off. Last week she had gotten a text with two words in caps that simply said CALL ME. Andrea had admitted to her mother that she was in the midst of a serious argument with Cam, but that was it. While her mother could make her call, she couldn't make her talk. Besides, she didn't want any more well-meaning advice. She wanted, no *needed* to figure this out on her own.

One lonely night, as she'd cried herself to sleep, the words of wisdom that her father had given her came to mind. She *did* believe that Camden was her real love. Her daddy was right, whoever didn't fight for real love when they found it were idiots. She was a lot of things, a little anal, a little reserved, but no one had ever called Andrea Cole an idiot. She knew what she wanted...she wanted Cam. Now she had to figure out how to get him back.

That was going to be the hard part. So she went into planning mode. She was going to treat this like one of her work problems. After all, she solved problems and made companies better on a regular basis. She had to figure out, what would make Camden believe she wanted him for the long haul? Once she started to think of her problem in business terms, a path forward started to become clearer.

It was late August and Camden was sitting in his house, drinking a beer. He'd finished his last project around three o'clock that day. He just needed to make another pass over everything before he sent it to the client tomorrow. Now that it was done, he could move on to thinking about Andrea twenty-four seven. She had reached out to him during the last week of July to ask if they could meet up and talk. Once again, he'd ignored her...and that had been the last time he'd heard from her. Almost a full month ago. Maybe Robert had been right. Maybe she'd given up. But didn't that confirm what he'd been trying to prove? That she didn't want this relationship as much as he did? That she wasn't willing to fight for it? It hurt and pissed him off that he'd put every single thing he'd had into building a relationship with her. After his parents' death, he'd never wanted to risk feeling the kind of pain of losing someone he loved. He'd taken a chance on Andrea. Was it so wrong of him to want the same from her?

During this last month, he had become resigned to the fact that it was basically over. He still felt that dull ache in his chest every time he thought about what they had, but conversely he also realized that he should have tried one more time to connect with her. It was true that maybe he'd jumped the gun on proposing. He hadn't talked to her directly about if she wanted to get married anytime soon, or what the path to marriage looked like to her. Robert was right, he'd hadn't wanted to accept anything less than her saying yes.

They could have talked about their differences and still been together. If he had given her a little more time...just a *little*, then maybe they could have reached a compromise. Instead, he'd drawn a hard line in the sand. He had wasted the countless times she had reached out to him. Now, he was spending all his nights alone, sitting in a house that still wasn't quite a home. If he had another chance...well he hoped like hell he wouldn't let his pride and bruised ego get in the way again.

Andrea's insight from the beginning of the month had put her on this current course of action. She had worked up the courage to do this all week long. She'd thought about waiting for Friday to arrive, but she was tired of the butterflies in her stomach. So, on Thursday after delaying at work, she found herself driving to Camden's house. She prayed the whole way there that he was at home, and more importantly, that he wouldn't slam the door in her face. She was on a mission to get her man back!

Pulling into his drive unleashed a lot of emotions as she saw the familiar house. It had become like a second home to her, she had missed being here. Parking the car, she made her way to the door. She was in a light summer dress and held a clutch purse in her hand. The only other thing she had was her courage. She gave the doorbell a long push and waited. He opened the inside door, only to gaze at her through the locked screen. When he didn't move or speak, she offered a small smile and asked, "Can I come in?"

Camden was shell-shocked. He had just been thinking about her, wishing he had another chance, and now she was on his doorstep. He was busy drinking her in. Another woman had never looked so good to him. He'd looked at pictures of her during the separation, but there was nothing like seeing her in the flesh. And just that quick, it was obvious another part of his anatomy besides his heart had missed her.

Opening the screen door, he said. "What are you doing here Andrea? And don't tell me you were just in the neighborhood."

"Okay...I won't. Can I come in? It's hot out here." She had been checking him out too, and he was still as fine as she remembered. She could tell he was still mad as well. While a part of her had known this wouldn't be easy, she wouldn't have minded him showing some enthusiasm upon seeing her.

"Fine." He stepped back so she could enter. "I suppose you're dying for some water as well. After all, we wouldn't want you getting dehydrated again, now would we?"

Andrea flinched at the reference to the night they'd split, squaring her shoulders even more she turned to face him in the hall. "Actually yes, a bottle of water would be good." As he veered off to the kitchen, she debated whether she should stand or sit. In the end, she took a seat on the couch.

Cam returned and handed her a cold water, eyeing her warily. He stood watching her take a sip while his mind ran a mile a minute. Why was she here now? He realized thus far, he'd been a bit of an asshole, but he had a lot of conflicting emotions going through him right now. Even so, he needed to calm down and not blow what might be their final chance of reconciliation. So it was a shock to him when this popped out his mouth. "So what? Are you here to return the ring?"

Andrea took another slow sip to settle her nerves. Is that what he wanted her to do? It was in her purse, in case he demanded it from her. Feeling tendrils of doubt enter her mind, she pushed them away. She was here to fight. If that meant fighting Cam to get what she wanted, what was best for them, then so be it. "Not quite...but I did want to give you this."

She pulled out the envelope from her purse with "return to sender" stamped on it, and handed it to him. He took it, sitting on the opposite edge of the couch. Looking at her before tossing the envelope carelessly on the table. When he just continued to look at her, she let a little of her own frustration come into her voice. "I got those range vouchers for *you*."

"And I wanted you to take me to the range. They should have been for *us*."

"They still can be Cam." Andrea softened her tone. "I would love for them to still be for us."

Cam lost his anger. Something about how she said his nickname always got to him. "Why are you here, Andrea? After two months?" He asked guardedly.

"The short answer...I love you." Before he could speak, she put up a hand to stop him. "I wanted to see you, but you ignored me. Why did you do *that* for two months?"

After a pregnant pause, he answered, "I did it because I'm a stubborn ass sometimes and because I'm a man...we have egos." When she gave him a sarcastic smile, he continued. "I love you too...I've missed the hell out of you."

"I've been pretty miserable without you." She moved closer to him. "I'm hoping we can talk, and work this out."

Cam nodded slowly. "I'd like that. Honestly, the first thing I need to know though, is why the thought of marrying me sent you into a panic?"

"For the same reason sleeping with you the first time had me trying to run. You make me feel things on a level I've never experienced before. You make me vulnerable in a way I'm not comfortable with. Feelings that I'm afraid to trust."

"I guess...I can understand that. But baby, you know I'd never hurt you."

"My head knows, but my heart knows that you have the *power* to do so. That wasn't the only reason. Before, with Damon, I had it in my head this 'plan' of what a relationship should look like. I'd meet a successful guy that treated me well and after a year of dating, he would propose. I expected Damon to fulfill this plan of mine on our one-year anniversary. As we sat in that fancy restaurant celebrating, my proposal never came. I was confused and angry and flat out told him what I was looking for."

Andrea paused and drank a bit more water as the feelings of disappointment, anger, and embarrassment rushed back to her. When she was steady, she looked into Camden's eyes before continuing. "He laughed at me, Cam. Said I was jumping the gun. He told me we had *potential*, but that he wasn't totally *sold* on me yet."

"That son of a-"

"No, let me finish. I told him that wasn't enough for me. That I had expectations of where this relationship was going. I thought stupidly, that he actually cared for me. He politely told me he couldn't make any promises and that on second thought maybe we weren't suited after all. That we were obviously not on the same wavelength. Basically, the same thing you told women that got serious about you."

"Andrea, you're different..."

"He took me home and that was that. He was done with me. Like the year I'd spent in his life meant nothing."

"Baby, I'm sorry. I bet what happened with us reminded you of all of that." Cam was kicking himself, for letting his boyish pride make him handle the engagement situation the way he had. He'd only compounded things when he'd ignored her time and time again. "I'm sorry he hurt you like that. I'm sorry *I* hurt you."

Andrea smiled sadly and shook her head. "Recently I realized I never loved him, just like he never loved me. News flash, women have egos too, and at the time, mine was crushed. It left me feeling insecure of my own judgement, of whether I would ever find what I wanted. What I *thought* I wanted...before I met you. So that's the long answer to your question about why I reacted how I did. I'm sorry I hurt you. I didn't mean to. It was never my intention."

"*I'm* sorry for being an insecure ass, and for how I treated you. I was putting my heart on the line for the first time with a woman, and I didn't like how it felt to be rejected. You were right, in that we never talked about marriage. That's my fault too. I was too much of a coward to broach it directly. Marriage is a big step that we should have considered together. I had it all settled in my mind and I just assumed you'd go along with it. I should have handled the entire situation from beginning to end better, and I regret that I didn't."

"Well...it looks like we both made mistakes. I'm here today hoping we can get past them. I miss being with my best friend."

"Same here." For the first time in months, Cam's genuine smile returned to his face. "I'm willing to let it go if you are."

"I am! But I do feel there is one more thing, I need to do before we can move forward." She reached back in her purse and pulled out a ring box. She saw uncertainty flicker across his face as he glanced at the box, then back to her. She flipped it open. "I got you a purple diamond, as well. Purple is the color of royalty. You have always treated me like a queen, and I want you as my king. Camden Joshua Holden, will you marry me?"

Camden looked down at the white-gold band that housed a purple diamond in the sunken center, two regular, smaller diamonds flanking either side.

With a light shining in his eyes that had been missing since walking out of her house, he gave a delighted laugh.

"I sure will baby. I love you Andrea." He pulled her in for a kiss, the first taste they'd had of each other in months. And just like the first time they had touched, electricity sparked through them. The simple kiss deepened, as their hands hungrily reacquainted themselves with each other, until they finally had to break apart to breathe.

"I've missed you...*us*," Andrea said quietly, stroking his jaw.

"So have I, pretty eyes. I don't want to be without you again. I'll marry you whenever, however you want. I don't care how long we wait, as long as we're together while we do."

A feeling of joy spread through Andrea and she kissed him again before saying the first thing that came to mind. "Let's get married now! Let's go to Vegas!"

Chapter Twenty-Six

Cam wondered if his hearing was off. He wouldn't be surprised if all his systems were out of whack, now that he had Andrea back in his arms. "Are you serious?"

"Yes! Why wait any longer? I bet we can catch a flight out tonight. It's only a little after seven. Are you in the middle of a big project?"

"No, I actually finished my latest one today. I need to do a final review, but that would just take me a few hours."

"Great! I have tons of time off. My boss reminded me of that when I was freaking out over you."

Now Cam grinned cockily. "I had you going crazy missing me huh?"

"Don't get a big head or I might take my ring back."

"Speaking of, hand it over so I can put it on."

Andrea did, and as he was slipping it on, she reached into her purse one final time and withdrew her own ring box. "Would you do the honors for me?"

When Cam saw what she held, the last little bit of tightness in his chest eased. "I'd love nothing more than to put this ring on your finger, Ms. Cole."

As he slid it on, she teased him. "Soon to be Mrs. Holden, if you're not to chicken to jump on a plane."

"Woman, that is one dare I have no problem taking. Do you want to head home and pack and I can meet you there?"

She reached out to entwine her hand with his, so that their rings touched. "No. From now on we do this journey together." She pulled him up and gave him a lingering kiss before walking with him to the stairs. "You go pack, then we'll head to my place. The airport is closer to me anyway."

"I love you so much right now...you think we got time to get a head start on the honeymoon?"

She laughed and pushed him towards the stairs. "No, you got twenty minutes to pack. While you're doing that, I'll use my laptop to book our flight."

Cam frowned and took a step back towards her. "I don't want you paying for the tickets."

"Give it a rest. I went to the same shop to get your ring. I *know* how much you paid for mine. You have no right to scold anyone about spending money. Go pack."

"Yes, ma'am. I better get used to giving in huh?"

"Well remember, happy wife, happy life. Now, get." Andrea watched him run up the steps before she burst into giggles and literally skipped out to her car to grab her work bag. Quickly booting up her laptop, she sent her boss a quick email letting him know she needed a week off. She explained that an urgent matter had come up, but that she would be available tomorrow morning by email to take care of any loose ends.

She couldn't believe she was being this impulsive, but it felt good, it felt right! She thought about her parents, but then pushed the worry aside. This was about her and Cam, it was *their* moment. She just knew she wanted to marry Camden, everything else could wait and sort itself out. By the time he came back down, she had booked their flights.

"I'm all set. Just got to grab my laptop and phone off the table here."

"Good. I booked us first class on the 10:15 flight out."

"Andrea..."

"Hush. I'm getting married, so yes, first class. I also grabbed us a suite at Caesars Palace. Unfortunately, we'll be getting in too late, to get our marriage license. However, they open up at eight and I pre-checked us in, so we should be fine."

"Damn, you did a whole lot in twenty minutes."

"I was motivated. Plus, you took twenty-five."

"My bad. Let me lock up the house and we can roll."

They raced to Andrea's house where she took thirty minutes to pack a bag. She thought she did an excellent job, considering a woman had more necessities to consider than a man, but she wasn't worried, as she could easily buy anything else she needed if she forgot something.

They made it to the airport a little after nine o'clock. After checking their bags, they proceeded to grab a quick bite to eat. Cam hadn't stopped touching her. Her arm, back, waist, anything he could reach since they'd left his house. He admitted to himself he didn't believe this was happening. So he had to touch her to reassure himself that it wasn't a dream. It was hard to believe he had woken up this morning thinking he'd never be in her life again, and now they were about to get hitched.

While they waited at the gate to board, they discussed their honeymoon. They decided they wanted to go someplace neither of them had ever been, but wasn't complicated to book quickly. Once they decided on Hawaii, he shot an email to his travel agent right before they boarded. Cam was positive his person would have options ready, first thing in the morning.

When the flight crew in first class found out they were newly engaged and on their way to get married, they received a shot out from the Captain. In the air Andrea pulled up the hotel wedding options, and they quickly picked out the Venus Garden. Andrea wanted an outside wedding. After that, Cam spent the remainder of the time reviewing his project. He would probably have to put in a couple more hours tomorrow, but this way he'd be ahead of schedule. They touched down around 11:45 pm Nevada time, so it was going on one in the morning by the time they got to their hotel and checked in. They were both beat and agreed to call it a night since they had to be up early the next day.

The next morning, they were up with the sun to go get their marriage license. They were called into the back fifteen minutes after arriving, and fifteen minutes after that, walked out with a legal license. On the taxi ride back to the hotel Andrea started to cry softly, but not softly enough that Cam didn't hear.

"Sweetheart what's wrong? Do you want to do this a different way? Are you missing having your parents here?"

"No, it's not that. I was reading that they can watch the ceremony live with an internet link. We can send it to my parents and your family in North Carolina." They had yet to notify a single soul they were jumping the broom, so to speak.

"Then what is it?"

"I just can't believe my best friend won't be here. I mean, we'll have a stranger standing up for us. That's the only part of this I don't like." Andrea wiped the few tears she'd shed off her face and squared her shoulders. "But I can deal with it. The ceremony is only a handful of minutes anyway."

"I feel you. I guess I always assumed Robert would be my best man, you know?" They were silent for a few moments and then Cam said, "What if we changed the wedding to Saturday evening and flew them out here? Would Mika come?"

Andrea picked up on his idea and approved. "It's Mika, so yes. Plus, if I spin it as 'broken hearted best friend has gone off the rails', she'll drop everything and come out. That's what a bestie does."

"Bet. Robert will fall for the same. He already thinks I'm a head case over you."

"Glad to know we both suffered. However, I'm more ecstatic we'll have our friends here to celebrate!"

Mika had gotten a text from Andrea around noon on Friday. Her friend claimed she had flown out to Vegas on a whim, as she just couldn't take thinking about Cam anymore. She of course agreed to fly out Saturday morning to join her. Which is how she found herself on this early-ass flight to meet up with her for breakfast.

As she smothered a yawn, Mika couldn't believe Andrea was so torn up that she basically ran away to the other side of the country. Did she ever want to fall in love so deep that it would hurt *that* much? She supposed she wanted love…just not all the drama that came with it. Who had time for that? Besides, this was about cheering up Andrea. She would get Andrea drunk and make sure she flirted with the cutest men in all the hottest clubs in Vegas. Mika had many talents, and one of them was being able to have a good time in any situation.

Settled on how she was going to drag Andrea out her funk, she took a look around the nearly empty first-class cabin. Andrea had insisted on paying and booking the short flight and she appreciated having more leg room this early in the morning. She was the only one in her two-person row and she had decided to stay in her window seat. Across the aisle from her was another single passenger.

It was a good looking brother sitting in the seat by the window as well. He was the color of dark chocolate, the kind she liked to eat to give herself an energy boost when she was running on fumes. He was sitting there in a three-piece day suit. He had on a pair of smart and if she had to admit it, sexy specs as he read a newspaper. Who the heck reads actual newspapers anymore?

She let her eyes take him in again and decided she didn't like what she saw. She worked with professional men day in and day out. Inside her creative marketing office, they wore high-fashion or casual suits. The clients she worked with were more likely to wear the stuffy kind of professional cut like the guy across from her. Mika owed her clients her healthy salary, but they were usually a pain in her butt. They lacked creative vision, which was why they hired her.

The black men she met in and out of work that looked like the guy sitting across from her were the worst. Usually, they were arrogant and boring. She could tell he thought he was self-important and high and mighty. Just the kind of man her mother would want for her. She tried to stay away from men like that, at all costs. Her free-spirited ways seemed to irk their nerves, and their constant serious nature made her feel hemmed in. She was the type of woman who would always need a little fun in her life. Speaking of fun, she hoped she and Andrea would find some men as fine as "Mr. Newspaper" to party with. *Only* if they were minus the superiority complex she felt her fellow passenger had.

Chapter Twenty-Seven

Andrea and Cam were sitting at a table in one of the hotel restaurants, waiting on their friends to arrive. They'd ordered some fruit, mimosas, and croissants to start. They had contacted the front desk earlier and knew that both Robert and Mika had checked in. Which meant they should be able to join them for the ten-thirty breakfast meeting.

Yesterday, the couple had spent the majority of the day making plans and talking. Cam put in another few hours finalizing his project, while she had touched base with her office, squaring away work for the next week. Then they had taken in Vegas, having fun and drinking in the sun. Reconnecting after the separation of the last two months.

When night fell, they both confessed to being semi worried about telling their friends their plans. They had high hopes that at the end of the day, their friends would be supportive. The worst-case scenario would be if one or both of them, were totally against it and refused to participate. Andrea and Camden were okay with that outcome as well. They were determined that nothing would keep them from getting married later today.

Andrea ate a few pieces of fruit. A satisfied smile on her lips as she thought back on last night.

"I don't want you worrying about what happens tomorrow, so stop stressing." Cam had kissed her. "I won't let anyone ruin our day." He took her lips again and eventually, she relaxed against him. "Let's turn in for the night. We have another early morning tomorrow. I'd try

to seduce you, but I bet you want to wait for your wedding night at this point."

"You thought wrong, Mr. Holden. Since I met a certain someone, I don't like to wait for anything anymore. Besides...I've really missed being with you."

"Well, if you're sure..."

"I'm positive. You need to start practicing your husbandly duty."

Grinning, Cam took hold of her again and they quickly spiraled into a feverish embrace. The taste of each other was so sweet after being apart for so long. Andrea ripped buttons off his shirt, trying to get to his skin. Her mouth soon followed what her hands had uncovered. How had she gone without his scent or the feeling of his arms around her, for two whole months? Never again, she promised herself.

"Damn, baby, I'm trying to go slow, but you not making this easy."

"I don't want slow...didn't I just say I'm not a fan of waiting?" To prove it, she had tackled getting his pants off, and in the next moment, they were naked. Her sundress had been easy to dispose of. When they crashed to the bed, Andrea had wrangled her way on top of him. She held his thick member in her hand and shivered at the soft feeling of his most private skin. She went to position him at her entrance and he put a hand on her waist.

"Baby...we need...a condom." Cam was panting like he'd ran a lap.

"Not tonight. I didn't stop taking my birth control." She eased just the tip of him inside of her, watching his gorgeous eyes glaze over. "I want to be with you...like this." She slowly eased down his entire length. That was the last thing slow to happen that night.

Camden had reached up to caress, squeeze, and massage her breasts as she rode him hard. The closer she *got to her climax, the wilder she got, digging into his abs for steadiness. Eventually, he had pulled her low to kiss her mouth as she ground her hips against his, going over the peak. He had barely let her recover before flipping her over and proceeding to take her as if his life depended on it. She had craved and loved every minute of it! They had gone at each other another time before finally falling asleep.*

Now as she thought back on it, she couldn't wait until their honeymoon! They'd always used condoms. However, back at the end January, once she had seen how much sex they were having, she had gone on birth control for double protection. They would probably continue to use one or both methods for a while. She had just wrapped her head around marriage, kids were a foreign thought for her at this point. She jerked to attention as Cam squeezed her leg.

"I bet I know what you were thinking about," Cam said with a chuckle.

"I'm just waiting on them to show up."

"You are a bad liar. You probably thinking about the same thing I am."

"And what would that be?"

Cam leaned even closer until he was able to talk into her ear. "I was remembering when you slid down my bare shaft, and how wet and hot you were. How I'd never felt anything so good! My eyes actually rolled into the back of my head! Almost got stuck from the way you rode me like a-"

"Cam!" She pushed him away, looking around to see if anyone else had heard his outrageous comments. That's when she noticed the greeter at the door pointing Mika in their direction. "Stop it, Mika's here!" She stood up and waved, even though Mika had already seen them in the small establishment.

By the time Mika made it over to the table, she was giving them a grim look. Putting one hand on her hip, she addressed them in a thoughtful tone. "Let me say up front, I'm flattered that you guys flew me out here to be your third. I know anything goes in Vegas, and usually, I'm all for it, but this time, I'm going to have to decline. I mean, you fine and all Cam, but you not worth losing my best friend over."

While Cam just laughed, Andrea reached out and gave her a little shove. "You are just as bad as him!" Before Andrea could say more, a voice spoke from behind Mika.

"Well...I wasn't expecting this."

Mika turned to see the man from the plane, up close and personal. He'd changed into more causal wear, but that didn't seem to diminish the air of arrogance that clung to him. "And who exactly are you?" she asked, unreasonably disturbed to see him again.

Robert flicked a quick glance down the front of her body. He had been behind her as they crossed the room. The woman had a well-rounded backside, that was for sure. Her face and chest were unexpectedly even better, though her attitude left a lot to be desired. "Robert...Robert Lorde, since you're asking."

"My man! You made it!" Cam interrupted their stare-off as he came around to give Robert a hearty hug. Andrea distracted Mika by giving her a hug of her own.

"Now that everyone is here, let's sit." Andrea gestured for everyone to sit down as she continued to babble. "We got some basics, but we can place a real order now if you want."

"Nice to see you again Andrea." Robert gave her a big genuine smile before turning to look at Cam. "What's going on here? Looks like you brought me out here on false pretenses."

Andrea grabbed Camden's hand nervously, on top of the table. She saw Mika's eyes shift to follow the gesture.

She figured she'd better rush to explain before Mika beat her to it. "We're getting married and we wanted our best friends by our sides. Surprise!"

When they were met with silence for a few seconds, Cam picked up the spiel. "What do you two think? Will you stand up with us when we get married today?"

Mika was the first to react letting out a squeal that had heads turning, before jumping up and launching herself at Andrea. "Of course I will! This is so amazing!"

Robert stood up as well giving Cam another hug, complete with back thumps. "Congrats my brother! I'm glad to see you came around and asked her to marry you again."

Cam was grinning ear to ear as he clarified. "It wasn't me. This time, she was doing all the asking."

Mika turned back to the men. "Wait, what? My cautious, overthinking Andrea proposed?"

"Yes. All of this..." Cam gestured to their surroundings. "Was her idea."

"Well getting *them* out here, was your original idea."

"True," Cam shot back.

"You two are nauseatingly cute," Mika cut in. "Sit down and explain how all this happened. I'm so excited, but I'm also a detail hoarder!"

They all set down and started to eat, finally calling the waitress over to place a more substantial order. Cam and Andrea told them about the events of the last two days, leading up to their decision to get married this evening at seven.

"This is awesome!" Mika exclaimed as they finished telling the tale. "The first wedding I'm going to be in!"

"What are you talking about? You were in your cousins' weddings."

Mika waved that pesky little fact away. "Fine, the first wedding of someone I actually *like* that I'll be in." Mika looked down at her phone and saw that it was almost noon. "We don't have much time. Do you have your colors picked out? Your dress?"

Andrea cut her exuberant friend off by grabbing her hand. "The venue is booked, the honeymoon is booked. I have everything I need, now that you're here."

Mika squeezed Andrea's hand. "Stop it! You're going to make me cry."

"Don't do that, save the tears for the ceremony. Confession time, I was hoping you would help me pick out a dress."

"Why would you save that for last? We have to go!" Mika tugged Andrea up.

Andrea looked at Cam helplessly. "I guess we'll meet up later." Scooping up her phone and purse, she added, "I'll text or call you with details, or if I need anything."

Mika was pulling her away from the table. "Girl come on and leave that man alone. We have work to do. You'll have the rest of your life with him, *if* we can find you a dress."

The two men watched as the women rushed towards the exit, Andrea waving at them over her shoulder as Mika dragged her along. Cam was laughing, while Robert shook his head, a little frown on his face. "She seems like a handful."

"Mika? Yeah, probably. Play nice, though. She's my future wife's BFF. They are extremely close."

Robert held up his hands. "Yeah, I remember you might have mentioned her a time or two. She's not my business...trust me, I plan to keep it that way."

"Good, I owe Mika. If it wasn't for her, it might have taken me several months before I got a real date out of my stubborn woman."

"I got you. Today will be about you two. So, anything we need to do on our end to make this happen?"

"Man, Andrea is an efficiency machine. You would appreciate her skills. We can go relax and live up my last day as a free man until Andrea sends me instructions."

"I see you already got 'staying out the way' like a husband down pat."

Cam smirked unabashedly. "You know it."

"Smart. I got breakfast. Think of it as a wedding gift. Let's pay, so I can buy you a drink in a strip club."

Andrea had shortlisted a few shops to look for something to wear. Las Vegas was definitely the city to do a wedding on the fly. They had many places that catered to both planned weddings and the last-minute folks like her. She wanted something light and not particularly traditional. She figured since she was going to Hawaii, they could hire someone to do some real wedding photos when they got to the tropical paradise. Therefore, she wanted to be able to wear the same dress.

They got lucky at the second place they went, when she found an empire-styled floor-length, chiffon dress in purple. It flowed around her, yet emphasized her breasts. Because it was sleeveless, the amethyst necklace Cam had given her would be front and center and would look lovely. It was kept from being extra simple by the color, which faded into lighter shades of purple in an ombré style, as it neared her feet. She loved it! For Mika, they found a sleeveless, short sheath dress with the same ombré colors, except they were going in the opposite direction. Mika insisted on taking a picture of Andrea's chest and sending it to Camden so he could coordinate some part of his and Robert's outfits to match.

"What did you do that for?" Andrea asked, snatching back her phone.

"To give him something to think about for the rest of the day. Besides, he can't see the whole dress. It's bad luck."

They moved on and finally found some white shoes that were neither flats nor stripper height. Seeing that it was nearing three o'clock, Mika dragged her back to the hotel and took her directly to the spa. At the register, she gave the clerk her credit card and looked back at Andrea. "My wedding gift to you. Can't have you out there on your honeymoon, walking the beaches with crusty elbows and feet."

"Hey, I take offense to that. I take care of my feet."

"Usually. But we both know you were letting a lot go over the last couple of months. This way Cam will get to enjoy soft, sexy skin all over." Turning back to the clerk, Mika continued, "Give me a simple mani and pedi. I need to change my nail color. Plus, a thirty-minute massage. Give her a full body treatment, a shellac mani and pedi, and the same massage. Oh, and get her some champagne...she's going to be a bride today."

"Cam had no problem with my skin last night," a chagrined Andrea mumbled under her breath before they were rushed off to their appointments.

By the time they finished it was after five. Mika convinced Andrea to get dressed in her room so that the first time Cam saw the dress would be at the wedding. She made sure he was still out and ran up to get the few things she needed. They planned to change after the wedding and go out to eat and celebrate, so she could pack everything then.

Cam had texted her about his outfit while she was in the middle of her massage. He and Robert would be wearing white linen summer suits with purple accents. She texted him the video link to send to his family and did the same for hers. That led to getting a phone call from her excited parents. They were thrilled for her, and of course upset they would miss the event, but they promised to be watching. Now with everything settled, she was tired. Mika noticed of course.

"Take a thirty minute nap. I have another quick thing I want to check downstairs, then I'll probably take one too."

"Good idea. My god Mika, I'm getting married!"

"I know. This is what you want, right?"

"It is. I've never been surer of anything before. I love him. Everything else will work out."

"I'm so glad you took this chance! I know you're going to be happy. You know that man loves you a lot. Now, go to bed, you making me cry again."

Andrea had wanted her wedding to take place right before sunset, which was a quarter after seven on this particular day. At seven on the dot, she found herself walking down the outside path in her purple dress, with a white bouquet. She knew that their friends were present. That there was a video camera somewhere, and a photographer who would try selling them pictures after the fact, but all she had eyes for was Cam. He was so gorgeous, and he was all hers.

She reached him and they held hands as he gave her his customary smile. They listened to the ordained minister go through the basic marriage ceremony. It seemed to be a blur of words that she barely heard over the pounding of her own heart. Her focus sharpened as the minister told Cam it was time for his vows.

"It hasn't escaped my notice that today is exactly a year from when we met last August. I knew you were going to change my life, when you looked up at me, with your pretty eyes on that sidewalk. Loving you has taught me patience, and to put someone else's needs before my own. It brings me incredible joy to make you smile, and I promise to always find new ways to do so. I know we have more things to learn about each other, and tribulations to overcome as well. More fun to be had and memories to be made. All those things I look forward to, as long as I get to do them with you. With you by my side, we'll make a house a home. I love you Andrea Renee Cole, and I can't wait to spend the rest of my life with you."

Andrea blinked fast to keep the tears at bay. Gripping his hand even harder, as it was her turn to share her heart.

"Camden Joshua Holden, running into you was the best thing that ever happened to me. I felt instantly that you were something special, which was why I tried to run the other way. I'm grateful you gave chase in the most romantic and caring ways possible. Over time, you became my best friend. I can't imagine my life without you in it, to tease me, reassure me and support me. I plan to do all those things for you as well. I love how you make me feel special and loved. I look forward to our specials outings, working late together and just snuggling on the couch with you. I don't ever want to *miss* you again, because I'll always be with you. You made me believe I could have a *real* love. I love you with everything I am, and neither of us will ever have to walk in this world alone again."

Epilogue

Snuggling into the warmth at her back, Mika tried not to wake up. She was so *not* a morning person. Squeezing her eyes shut, she slowly let her mind come awake. She felt good, relaxed, and her body had that low-key hum that only great sex gave her. Speaking of sex...something big and hard was pressed against her bottom. She gave a satisfied smile in her semi-sleep state for about three seconds before her eyes popped open.

Wait just a damn minute...she hadn't had sex in almost five months. So who the hell nice sized penis was rubbing up against her? Hell, where *was* she? Mika snapped her eyes closed again and held still, hoping the man sharing the bed would remain unaware that she was woke. She dug deep and processed her memory banks.

Okay what is the last thing you remember? Umm a flight? Yes! Yes, a flight! And just like that, the puzzle pieces started to click into place, playing like a slideshow in her brain. She had come to Vegas for what she thought was a spur of the moment trip, meant to cheer up her best friend. Then, she had been blindsided by Andrea saying she was getting married and standing up for her in the wedding. That was as far as she got before the memories trailed off. Who the hell was in her bed? Were they even in *her* bed, or were they in *his*? She had been accused of being a free spirit from time to time, and Vegas was Vegas, but this was taking it a bit far!

She didn't even know anyone in Vegas, besides Andrea and Cam and...oh no. She jerked up, pulling the sheet up to her breasts like some self-conscious, proper lady from the 1950s, and glared at her bed partner. *"You!"*

Robert, who had barely missed getting chin-checked as she flung herself up, just rolled his eyes and felt his morning wood disappear. Looking at her, he stated, "Let me guess...you're not a morning person?"

You can download a book club discussion guide for *Running Into You* at: www.TaylorMadeDaydreams.com

**Join us for the next book in the
"Instant Chemistry Series"
Coming Fall 2018!
Taylor Love**

Not My Type

Their best friends may be married, but no law said *they*
have to like each other.

Mika lives the saying "carefree black girl" to the fullest.
She has a solid interesting career, good friends, and money
to do whatever she wants! What she doesn't have is a man
of her own. Even so, she's not so desperate that she'll
fall for Robert Lorde. While he may be tall, dark, and
handsome, he's way too arrogant and boring to be her type.

Robert likes his life to be predictable. While others see
that as boring, he counts his blessings for the stability. As a
financial investor, the last thing he needs is whirlwind Mika
Harrison tearing through his life. Yet even his practical
mind can't deny the chemistry they have. Will a little
fun with her leave him with a headache...or even worse, a
heartache?

About the Author

Taylor Love is a new author who calls Michigan her home. An avid reader since she was a young girl, she gained a love of writing as well. She loves to read a variety of genres and hopes over time to expand her writing among several of them. She is a lover of learning a "little bit" about many things. She hopes her imagination brings her readers a few hours of enjoyment!

Books by Taylor Love
Running Into You